An Atheist's Letters to Heaven

An Atheist's Letters to Heaven

Naimbai Njerakey

RESOURCE *Publications* · Eugene, Oregon

AN ATHEIST'S LETTERS TO HEAVEN

Resource Publications
An Imprint of Wipf and Stock Publishers
199 W. 8th Ave., Suite 3
Eugene, OR 97401

www.wipfandstock.com

PAPERBACK ISBN: 978-1-7252-7793-9
HARDCOVER ISBN: 978-1-7252-7794-6
EBOOK ISBN: 978-1-7252-7795-3

Manufactured in the U.S.A.   06/23/20

Contents

Acknowledgement

I am deeply indebted to my Creator—the source of my life and strength—the Inspiration behind this book, and the One who employed me as a mere penman in crafting this novel. I wonder sometimes what a depraved, vile sinner as I have done to deserve the love, grace, mercy, and attention of God. He has indeed saved me, called into the ministry, and laid the desire to pen this book in my heart. Countless a time I have failed Him in my sin, doubt, and rebellion but He is always there for me in my lowest points in life, in solitude, and in times of well-deserved trial. I am grateful that my Maker speaks to my rebellious, stubborn conscience until I lament over my offenses (sin) against Him and seek reconciliation in prayer. Without Jesus Christ, I seriously doubt that I would be here today—not just because the only begotten Son of God lived a sinless life, shed His blood, died, and resurrected three days later to atone for my sins and restore the severed relationship with the Father—but the name of Christ keeps me going in turbulent, stormy times and gives me intrinsic value when no one seems to care. I am also thankful for my family, especially my father Dasnan and mother Bonodji who have been my most loyal earthly supporters since day one. They made tremendous sacrifice to send me to school, bring me to the United States, and support my decision to serve the Lord—and continue to make sacrifice for me today. May God reward them according to His divine will and timing. I would like to express my gratitude to my skilled editor, Rebecca Faith and beta reader, Jessica Houdart, without whom, humanly speaking, this project wouldn't come to fruition. Special thanks go to my host family (the Covington's) for being my reliable, faithful family in America and my cousin Jean-Paul Koualaou who was very encouraging in the writing of this book. Thank you Open Door Baptist Church for being my church family. May God reward my friends who encouraged me in the writing process and have been praying for the materialization of this book. My gratitude also goes to Dr. Guiler for endorsing this book. Lastly, thank you to all the readers of this novel. Your feedback is invaluable.

1

Marawi and Melchizedek's Providential Reunion

Monday, March 8, 1993
1939 Bemba Road
Kamda, Earthly Domain

Dear Brother Melchizedek,

I am penning this letter to express my gratitude to you for revealing your mailing address in the vision I had last week and to ask a few questions regarding spirituality. I miss you dearly and do not go a day without reflecting on our temporary but extremely agreeable time together when you were still a part of what you often referred to as "fleeting, mundane life." Before passing away, you were steadfast in your effort to convince me to have a so-called "personal relationship with God the Father through Jesus Christ his Son." I neither took your arguments with any degree of seriousness, nor thought I would be able to communicate with you once death parted us. Recent unprecedented events and an ongoing realization of ample flaws in scientific theories have defied my worldview and shaken my faith in science.

I am astounded to discover that the revered entity that you referred to as God revealed himself to me when I challenged him to do so—just like you told me. He informed me that you will, henceforth, serve as a means of communication between us, and that I have the discretion to pose any question that my heart desires as I embark on this journey to discover what is "truth." Further, I was instructed in the vision to leave my letters between the sycamore and cedar trees located behind my house. A supposed archangel named Michael will be dispatched periodically to carry my note to you in the afterlife and return your response at a convenient time.

Although the vision did not affect my resolve to remain a staunch atheist, I am now, however, willing to hear arguments that support your worldview, because you always attempted to provide coherent, comprehensive responses regarding the profound questions of life—namely, origin, meaning, morality, and destiny—based on the Judeo-Christian worldview.

Dear friend, I do not wish to bother you any further with this present note, but I expect a response from you in the near future. Be sure to let me know whether you want to have an honest, open discussion regarding the true meaning of life.

Regards,
Your friend, Marawi

Monday, April 12, 1993
1517 Year Zero BCE Road
Paradise, God's Kingdom

My Dear Brother Marawi,

I, your friend, Melchizedek, am very blessed to have known you when I was not a part of the world you referred to as the "state of nothingness." I am especially grateful to the Almighty for making me your soulmate on earth. During my days with you, you shared with me the heartbreaking and unfortunate loss of your mother at such a young, tender age. Death is misconceived by most humans, who fear the inevitable transition from the corrupted, fleeting world to purified eternity. Because I too am deceased, I can tell you with unerring certainty that I recently spoke with your mother on a street of Paradise. She trusts that you will ultimately triumph both in faith and vocation. Which brings me to the motive of my letter: The Lord has a message for you concerning the direction of your life and the trajectory that your eternal soul is on.

God, the Creator of the universe; the omniscient, omnipresent, and omnipotent; the one who knows the depths of your heart and life; and the one who affirmed "I am Alpha and Omega, the beginning and the end, the first and the last,"[1] loves you unconditionally and eternally. Indeed, the Father knows that you have a low self-esteem and are somewhat displeased with yourself. Although you are a distinctively fine and rigorous young man, you have always seen yourself as unattractive and unworthy of life. Dear friend, self-love is indispensable in loving your fellow human beings and developing a meaningful, lasting relationship with the Creator. You must distinguish between pride and genuine self-love, which does not boast but is rather expressed outwardly through the love of your fellow human beings. I am not demanding an immediate outpouring of love here, but you must not become the victim of those who speak against you, for out of their mouths come hurtful and untrue statements that in turn shape your self-concept. They don't know you, those who seek to bring about your downfall through verbal abuse and cunning actions; you are fearfully and wonderfully made in the image of God.[2] The Lord knew you before you were conceived in your mother's womb, just like the prophet Jeremiah.[3]

True love has no external origin apart from the Lord: It begins with one's realization that he or she is created by the most supreme force in the universe, and there is an unbridled relationship between Creator and creation. The Creator's transcendent love is clearly spelled out in Genesis when Moses affirmed, "In the day that God created man, in the likeness of God made he him."[4]

The unpleasant truth is that a world wherein everyone is treated with flawless dignity and respect remains an imaginary and elusive utopia apart from the kingdom of heaven. From the time Adam walked upon the face of the earth, mankind has been striving to achieve a universal notion of human rights and the so-called perfect society. Kings issued vain edicts in this regard, and contemporary politicians institute laws to no avail. The problem, though often denied and overlooked, is because God is kept out of the various solutions proposed to find a cure for the never-ending cycle of universal inequality and injustice. Society would improve if man remembers that life is sacred and man's dignity is esteemed by God such that he commanded: "Whoso sheddeth man's blood, by man shall his blood be

---

1. Revelation 22:13 (KJV).
2. See Genesis 1:26–27; Psalm 139:14.
3. See Jeremiah 1:5.
4. Genesis 5:1 (KJV).

shed: for in the image of God made he man."[5]Objective concepts of human dignity and rights are meaningless without God.

The Father, therefore, commands that you remain unheeding and unyielding against negative and inconsiderate comments. As I mentioned before, you are fearfully and wonderfully made in the image of God and are blessed with incredible, unmatched, and untapped talent. At an appointed time, the Almighty is going to use what he has stored in you to help humankind come to repentance and have communion with him at the place he prepared for the elect.

I must share what I went through during my earthly life and its ramifications after I departed the land of men. While growing up in southern Lebanon, I was a subject of much taunting and was an object of scorn in the eyes of my peers—and sadly of loved ones as well. This fact, combined with my somewhat timid demeanor, made it extremely difficult for me to make and keep friends. My perceived isolation increased to the point that it was not only an internal struggle, but also forced me to totally shut myself off from society. I became a sociopath and an introvert who shunned his fellow human beings. Thus, through much of my early youth, I was a virtual antisocial recluse, desirous of vengeance and mischief. My life got worst when both of my parents lost their lives in a shipwreck en route to the Republic of Chad in central Africa to speak at a conference. The tragic voyage, in which, by the grace of God I was absent due to school, took me by surprise, left me in shock, and made me an orphan overnight. Nonetheless, the incident opened my eyes to reality and compelled me to gradually accept people into my life. In time, I was radically changed by those I met along the journey to become a sociable person once again, and God utilized my newly established friendship with the Covington family to reveal one important lesson to me: true joy is only found in him through the death of his Son Jesus Christ at Calvary. What I want you to retain from this story is this: Never let negative comments or lamentable circumstances rule over your life and affect your view of God. See yourself the way God sees you.

Beloved Marawi, meditate on God's words to the children of Israel while they sojourned in the wilderness, prior to their entrance to the Holy Land: "Thou shalt love the Lord thy God with all thine heart, and with all

---

5. Genesis 9:6 (KJV).

thy soul, and with all thy might."[6]Should you heed this command, self-love and the love of mankind would naturally follow.

My friend, your soul is marred and tarnished by sin because of your continual rejection of the truth: you can indeed be forgiven, and once you receive Jesus Christ as your Lord and Savior, your actions and attitude toward life will drastically change forever; for you shall set your eyes on the things in God's kingdom and imitate the life of the Son rather than being burdened with mundane preoccupations.

I am confident you will ponder the advice inspired by God herein and embark on a spiritual journey to know the Lord. Your mother and I trust that you will slowly but surely move away from your sinking, blinding, atheistic views and give your life to Christ. We are confidently optimistic and are fervently passionate for your soul to be with us one day. Be sure of one thing, however, the ultimate decision rests with you.

I expect further inquiries from you soon and am eager to carry on this discussion.

Love,
Your friend and brother, Melchizedek

6. Deuteronomy 6:5 (KJV).

2

God, Love, Sin, Purpose, Righteousness

Saturday, May 1, 1993
1939 Bemba Road
Kamda, Earthly Domain

Greetings my friend!

I am delighted to receive your reply and confirmation to correspond. I appreciate your reaffirmation of our genuine, mutual brotherly love but dismiss your fantasy regarding my mother. It is inconceivable to imagine two complete strangers meeting one another in another dimension after death. I urge you to keep your fantasies to yourself. My mother was never the type of mother I wished to have. She did not let me live life in my own way, and always tried to force religion upon me. I enjoy life to the fullest and care less about what she referred to as sin. I create my own reality, and do not let a so-called God or religion dictate my life because I have total control of my life; professional success that you call vocation will be achieved from my own effort and sweat—not providence. Therefore, make no mistake, I am indeed on a path to gain renown among my coworkers, family members, friends, and beyond.

I want to know the author of the outrageous phrase, "Thou shalt love the Lord thy God with all thine heart, and with all thy soul, and with all thy might." Who does he think he is? What gave him the prerogative to say such a thing? What are his qualifications and credentials? I am an independent man and thinker with a free will to do as I see fit. Even if my mother exists in the metaphysical dimension you speak of, you two better find something more fulfilling to do than caring for me. Know one thing: It did not, is not, and will not work.

I laugh to scorn the presumed fact that your God has the audacity to say that he knows the depths of my life and heart. How can an educated, rational person espouse the notion that there is a certain *Being* up in the sky who determines the happenings of the universe and is aware of the inner thoughts of men?

Dear Melchizedek, I am frankly disappointed and feel insulted by the unthoughtful words you utter concerning the present state of my soul—if there is such a thing. I am in no need of forgiveness because I am a good, honorable citizen who makes tremendous sacrifice for his family and humanity. I do not kill, steal, or earn money dishonestly. In fact, you are the one who should apologize for advancing such offensive falsehoods. I am, however, appreciative of you sharing the anecdote. I dislike the conclusion but can relate to your story because of the untimely death of my mother and the mockery I am often subjected to.

I expect more entertaining fables from you soon.

Sincerely,
Njerabé Marawi

Monday, June 7, 1993
1517 Year Zero BCE Road
Paradise, God's Kingdom

Dear friend,

T hank you for your response. I enjoyed reading your thoughtful words and would like to clarify the points I made in my previous letter. First, dear friend, I did indeed meet your mother—I penned no fiction. Consider the following words in the Bible: "For God commanded, saying, Honour thy father and mother: and he that curseth father or mother, let him die the death."[1] Therefore, be very careful how you refer to your mother and speak of her. Are you confused regarding the excerpt, "Thou shalt love the Lord thy God with all thine heart, and with all thy soul, and with all thy

1. Matthew 15:4 (KJV).

might?" You openly challenged this commandment while not realizing that you have subconsciously surrendered already to another god—the god of self, perpetuated by pseudoscience. Indeed, the underlying reason for the sustained rejection of Christianity, which most unbelievers refuse to admit publicly, stems from the misconception that Christianity is a controlling religion that demands absolute, blind loyalty and submission to God, thereby trampling on individual liberties. People typically enjoy sinful leisure such as drinking, going to nightclubs, cheating on their spouse, enriching themselves dishonestly, and using profanity. Since God commands those who follow him to avoid seeking pleasure in these things, unsaved individuals view Christianity as a threat to their lifestyle. What they fail to understand is that godlessness leads not to freedom but rather to enslavement to the vices of the world. The lost may experience happiness in sin but not true joy which can only be found in Christ. The above commandment has no other author besides God. He gave it to the children of Israel just before the Ten Commandments. It still applies to life today. Your simple mind does not comprehend the depth of God's infinite love and his unwavering mercy that extends to you. It is his unconditional love that led him to take human form and die on the cross for sinners. He is the same God whose spiritual love is far greater than human love, and commanded humans to love their enemies, neighbors, and strangers.[2] You claim to be independent and a free thinker, but you are undoubtedly selective in what you consider free thinking.

You have a great deal of pride and self-righteousness (no need to ask for forgiveness), and your primary objection to recognizing sin—like other unbelievers—is the misconception that admitting this reality would curtail your liberty, giving you a false sense of limitation on your freedom. Jesus Christ said to the Jews that believed in him, "If ye continue in my word, then are ye my disciples indeed; And ye shall know the truth, and the truth shall make you free."[3] I can attest to this fact as a born-again Christian who has been set free from the bondage of sin. Let me reassure you that a relationship with Christ—hence, communion with God—is not designed to keep one in bondage but rather to free one from the shackles of sin. A life without God is a life in bondage, whether or not a person knows it. Brother Marawi, you are a slave to sin and are indeed not free, and like other sinners, you are slave to the idols of pornography, the quest for fame,

2. See Matthew 5: 43–44; Luke 10: 25–37

3. John 8:31–32 (KJV).

an unrestrained search for sexual gratification, swearing, nightclubbing, gossiping, adultery, blasphemy, and hate—just to name a few. I recommend that you look at your life in retrospect and see how these vices have kept you in bondage and led you to a permanent state of depression. It is your pride that makes you reject God and seek alternate sources of joy.

Your erotomania and desire for renown (fame) among men should point you to the Creator, who alone can make you whole. Dear friend, the truth of the matter is that man's heart is insatiable, and this fact points him to a greater longing and purpose—a longing that can only be fulfilled by the grandest and most supreme power in the universe. Pride and arrogance make you claim that you create your own reality and have total control over your life, with no concern for the gravity of sin. The Word of God says, "If we say that we have no sin, we deceive ourselves, and the truth is not in us. If we confess our sins, he is faithful and just to forgive us our sins, and to cleanse us from all unrighteous. If we say that we have not sinned, we make him a liar, and his word is not in us."[4] Both believers and unbelievers sin, but what sets them apart is found in 1 John 2: "My little children, these things write I unto you, that ye sin not. And if any man sin, we have an advocate with the Father, Jesus Christ the righteous: And he is the propitiation for our sins: and not for ours only, but also the sins of the whole world. And hereby we do know that we know him, if we keep his commandments."[5] Admission of sin and realization of one's depraved condition is the difference, my friend.

To illustrate the subtlety and gravity of sin, examine the words of Jesus found in Matthew 5: 21–30. This biblical passage accurately demonstrates the severity of sin and how subtle it can be sometimes. Jesus didn't only speak of the sins of action, but also the sins of thought. Self-righteous individuals blunder because they fail to grasp that there is not only sin of commission but also that of intention: they tend to minimize wicked thoughts and the nefarious devices of the mind and heart. I used to think like you: I do not steal, kill, or earn money dishonestly . . . But when I got saved and started to walk close with God, I realized that he is the ultimate embodiment of holiness, perfection, and justice. I began to see my heart and actions in a way I have never seen them before. One cannot be saved and walk closely with God and still say that he is good, for it is the work of the devil to keep the unsaved blind to their depravity and need. It is only through

4 1 John 1:8–10 (KJV).

5. 1 John 2:1–3 (KJV).

the atoning blood of Jesus Christ that justification can be attained. Needless to say, the human perception of good is often done with evil intent; as the prophet Isaiah rightly puts it: "But we are all as an unclean thing, and all our righteousnesses are as filthy rags; and we all do fade as a leaf; and our iniquities, like the wind, have taken us away."[6]

Beloved brother, you consider yourself righteous based on what society considers moral or immoral, but there is no small sin in the eyes of God. Indeed, sin does not require action or demand tangible manifestation. It can simply be a thought or series of thoughts. In the latter part of the aforementioned passage, Jesus Christ spoke metaphorically to instruct those who fear (reverentially respect) God to forsake things that cause them to sin, rather than clinging to them; for the end thereof is eternal damnation and separateness from the Lord. I urge you, beloved Marawi, to let go of your false sense of self-righteousness and justification, lest you be cast into hell fire when you stand in judgment before God. Whether you believe in a Creator or not, you cannot guarantee your next breath. You're still living by the grace of God, not because you have control over your life and destiny. As our Creator, the Almighty can choose at any moment to take your life. Humble yourself and turn away from the path of wickedness and perdition. Don't commit the same mistake as Belshazzar the Babylonian king who despised God and thought that he had control over his life but lost it abruptly when God, in whose hand was his breath, decided to take it back.[7]

A wise person learns and changes and I trust that you will do likewise.

Cordially yours,
Your Brother, Melchizedek

Thursday, June 17, 1993
1939 Bemba Road
Kamda, Earthly Domain

Melchizedek,

I appreciate you clarifying the previous remarks you made concerning my mother, love and the so-called sin, though I categorically disagree

6. Isaiah 64:6 (KJV).
7. See Daniel 5.

10

with everything you said. I will continue to be the master of my life, think that I am a good, honorable citizen, and disregard what you term sin, which in reality is a guise for me to accept your fictitious deity. My life is complete and adherence to Christianity guarantees less personal contentment. Be assured that I have absolute control of life at the moment—a belief in your Christ would reduce the contentment and fulfillment of the status quo. The fact that you listed things that might be a part of my daily habit to justify your point that I am in "a state of servitude" is untrue and inconsiderate. As far as I am concerned, my life is blameless, and although I enjoy watching pornography, lying, and stealing once in a while, these acts are part of my freedom and personal life. I am not enslaved to them! On the contrary, you appear to promote polytheism by asserting that gratifying hobbies such as sex, nightlife, and the pursuit of riches that humans enjoy, unknowingly constitute the demigods of their life. I unapologetically take pride in enjoying the things that you call gods and am in no way slave to them. In contrast, you were a slave to your God while living because you were brainwashed to abstain from these deeply gratifying hobbies. I recall us being companions in doing the things you called "gods of unsaved men" prior to your conversion to Christianity. Dear friend, let me reassure you that you acted foolishly in this regard and missed out on a life that could have been far more fulfilling and enjoyable.

Allow me to offer my counter-perspective to the points you raised concerning love, fame, pleasure, and joy. Indeed, you offended me by assuming that I lack the mastery of primary school vocabulary by lecturing me on the difference between joy and happiness. Indeed, I am aware of the difference between being happy and being joyful. To cope with my chronic struggle with depression, I hired a team of psychologists and a yoga teacher to help me achieve the coveted state of satisfaction, irrespective of my mental, financial, and physical state—commonly referred to as *joy*. The team of highly trained professionals that I hired has incorporated elements of Eastern philosophy and scientific theories to guide me into the noble life objective of joy. Although costly, I've seen considerable improvement in the way I view life and how I approach problems. Furthermore, you erred in making the foolish assumption that I am a prideful person and it is because of my pride that I reject your God and seek alternative sources of joy. Dear friend, I am frankly outraged by your continuous moronic presumptions, especially coming from you, who knew me very well for a very long time. If this is what you define as *prideful*, then I am indeed proud of being prideful.

I refuse to look at my life in retrospective because it is counterproductive to my effort to move forward. Although I am willing to concede that my past life is full of bitterness and regrets, I don't think it was a result of being proactive and not submitting my will to the authority of your God. I hold a simple philosophy when it comes to coping with the past: embrace my failures and concentrate all my efforts on future successes.

I cannot quite grasp the concept of the infinite love of your God and his unwavering mercy—a supposed love that led him to take human form and die on the cross for sinners. This notion is simply not in line with my atheistic beliefs. I am taught in my society to be independent and to never beg someone for pity. Mercy, the way I see it, is temporary and contingent upon certain terms. Under no circumstance would I let myself believe that a God I did nothing for would have unconditional mercy and love for me. I am free to love whoever I want to, and love is a manifestation of an affection that necessitates the existence and presence of two individuals. How can I love and submit to an unseen and nonexistent being? I love my wife and children just fine without having to love your God. I shall, by no means let myself be persuaded by your groundless and foolish advice. Conversely, I am amused by your pitiful attempt to diminish my self-esteem when you say that I should love my neighbor—a stranger with whom I have no business—as myself. This is the most absurd and selfish thing I have ever heard! Here in the West, we are taught from a young age to be independent and love people only after we know them and expect something in return. At times, individuals from the same family grow up to disdain each other, not to mention strangers. Life has taught me that showing affection to people without merit constitutes a recipe for disaster. Have you ever heard of the phrase, "taking advantage of someone"? Well, that's what happens to those who have an unconditional love for strangers. I have witnessed the abuse of unrestrained love firsthand in the lives of my Christian friends who are repeatedly taken advantage of by strangers with whom they have no business. The noble truths of the survival of the fittest and the theory of evolution have taught us humans to avoid this very mistake. These theories encourage us to strive for self-preservation, even at the expense of other people; self-preservation is of essence. We (humans) live in a mean and nasty world that has no place for the meek and lowly like you. I proudly inform you, therefore, that I will never love my neighbor or a stranger, for the person who matters is Marawi.

Likewise, you naively assume that spiritual love is far superior to real tangible love. I do not understand in what way or manner this would be possible. Human-to-human love is far more powerful and meaningful on so many levels. First, the concerned parties (individuals) are present. They can see one another, touch each other, laugh together, and face the challenges of life together. Second, genuine human love is expressed directly (face to face) rather than through vain prayers and repetitions. The latter point bears a special significance because one knows exactly who is professing and showing the affection. Third, it is much easier to hold a person accountable and evaluate their affection in a human-to-human love, unlike spiritual love that is vain and abstract, with no accountability between the god(s) and their so-called worshippers. Having said that, I highly doubt that my life and the way I love my wife and children would drastically change should I convert to Christianity. There is absolutely no supporting evidence regarding this claim, and I strongly believe that the contrary would likely happen.

Last, you cited fame along with the quest for sexual gratification to justify the reality of an unsatisfiable desire that your God placed in man. I cannot differ more on this point because there is no such thing as an insatiable desire in humans. I, however, suspect you are attempting to borrow from the great Buddha, who once made the assertion that the suffering that people experience in life is a direct result of their desires that cannot be quenched. For logic's sake, why wouldn't one set his sight on fame? Given that there is no afterlife, my primary goal is to enjoy life to the fullest and gain as much renown as possible among my fellow humans before death knocks at my door. Although you will evidently disagree with me on this point, it is this very conviction that forces me not to even fathom the idea of becoming a Christian, for it is a religion that does not promote or encourage the quest for self-excellence and the indulgence of pleasure. My motto is not "glory to God in the highest," but "glory to Marawi, the powerful human in the highest."

I chose to end the letter on these notes.

Bye!
Marawi

Friday, June 25, 1993
1517 Year Zero BCE Road
Paradise, God's Kingdom

Brother Njerabé,

You have greatly erred in saying that your life is complete and adherence to Christianity guarantees less personal contentment. Your perception of happiness defines the very difference between happiness and joy: joy is a permanent state of satisfaction, regardless of one's circumstances. Unlike happiness, which is conditional and temporal, true joy can only be found in the Lord and is everlasting. When a person leans on the Lord during the lows and highs of life, that dependency creates a continual state of joy. The Scriptures assert that the pride of the arrogant brings their downfall.[8] I am, therefore, concerned that you are allowing yourself to make the same mistake that the proudhearted and the stiff-necked make. What are your deepest desires? Do pornography, lying, and stealing give you lasting joy? Do you truly believe that the mundane way of happiness provides an answer to the deepest longings of the heart? When was the last time you heard of a human who quenched his thirst and desire for sexual intercourse, money, fame, or materialism? Consider what Jesus said in the parable of the wheat and the tares and see if you are not allowing yourself to make the same mistake: "He also that receiveth seed among thorns is he that heareth the word; and the care of this world, and the deceitfulness of riches, choke the word, and he becometh unfruitful."[9]

You also misdefined love and forgot its original significance. Indeed, love does not require two individuals in a physical sense. For instance, you tend to still love your mother and me, although we are no longer alive visibly in your domain. This reality alone should make you aware that love is a condition of the heart, expressed overtly and internally. The problem with atheists is that they think humans are unidimensional. For them, the physical body is all that there is. Humans are tridimensional, consisting of the body (physical), the spirit, and the soul (mind, emotion, will). Further, God designs each person with a void and a longing to seek and commune with him. I am sure you can attest to this fact on a personal level since you expressed the desire to search and know the truth. Once you give your life

8. See Proverbs 16: 18.
9. Matthew 13:22 (KJV).

to Jesus Christ, you will come to realize that love does not require the physical presence of two or more individuals but can also be metaphysical and transcendent. In fact, spiritual love is far more powerful and deeper than temporal, and often conditional, human-to-human love. You love your wife and children, and I commend you on this. In fact, the duty of every married man is to honor the sacred ordinance ordained by the Father, that is, to love one's wife as one's self.[10] However, once you love God and have a personal relationship with him, your relationship with your wife and children will change for the better and will be enriched in ways that you never imagined.

Indeed, you are free to love whoever your heart desires, but you must know that true, meaningful, lasting love starts with a personal relationship with God. Children with loving parents grow up and tend to be far more loving to others than children who did not have loving parents. Likewise, if you want your love for others to be more meaningful, you ought to have a relationship with Jesus Christ. He is the one who commanded, "Love your neighbor as yourself."[11] This is the love that Christ spoke of when he said, "But I say unto you, Love your enemies, bless them that curse you, do good to them that hate you, and pray for them which despitefully use you, and persecute you; That ye may be the children of your Father which is in heaven: for he maketh his sun to rise on the evil and on the good, and sendeth rain on the just and on the unjust. For if ye love them which love you, what reward have ye? do not even the publicans the same?"[12] If this seemingly simple, yet very important commandment is observed by humans, most of the so-called modern plights of man would be nonexistent. If one loves his neighbor as himself, he would not rob or slander him; if one loves his neighbor, he would not murder him or commit adultery with his wife; if one loves his neighbor, he would not oppress him, and so forth. The love of God entails far more than the limited human mind can comprehend—the love of God surpasses all love, defies human logic, and is simply incomprehensible.

Whether you suffer emotionally or from a bad experience, look to the unconditional love of God—take heart and get on your knees—take the matter to the Lord in prayer.

I wish you well.
Melchizedek

10. See Ephesians 5: 25–33 (KJV).
11. See Mark 12:31.
12. Matthew 5: 44–46 (KJV).

An Atheist's Letters to Heaven

Sunday, July 4, 1993
1939 Bemba Road
Kamda, Earthly Domain

Bro. Melchizedek,

I appreciate you taking the time to thoroughly read my note and attempt to reply to the points I raised. My view on the controversies we discussed—sin, pleasure, and the attitude toward my mother—has not changed. The point you made regarding love not requiring the presence of two individuals caught my attention, however, for I never figured out why I love my mother and you, though both of you are deceased. As for the tridimensional nature of humans (body, spirit, and soul), I came to an inconclusive conclusion. On one hand, science is a field that gives a certain degree of validity to any hypothesis until proven noncredible. On the other hand, claims advanced without following the scientific method are rejected.

How can you preach about God, or Creator of all things, as you call him? There is no such thing! No single theory or worldview can offer a credible explanation for creation of the universe. I am a firm believer in the big bang theory, as well as evolution, naturalism, and natural selection. I, therefore, reject the notion of a single, unified supreme force in the universe. I am created after the image of nothing and no one, apart from being a product of evolution and natural selection—time plus matter plus chance. If there is a God, who created him? Given the extensive confusion surrounding your mythical belief, the concept of sin simply does not exist in my world, and nothing limits my freedom, save the dictates of science.

As for me, fame, comfort, education, and money define success and fulfillment in life—not the love of your God. Professional success is not possible without these things. Given that there is no afterlife, my primary goal is to enjoy life to the fullest and gain as much renown as possible among my fellow humans before death knocks at my door. Although you will likely disagree with me on this point, it is this very conviction that makes the idea of becoming a Christian unfathomable, for it is a religion that does not promote or encourage the quest for self-excellence and the indulgence of pleasure. My motto is not "glory to God in the highest" but "glory to Marawi, the powerful human in the highest."

I expect you to provide clarification about kneeling to an imaginary God instead of commending me on my commendable character: I am good, honorable citizen who makes unimaginable sacrifices to serve his community and country. I do not steal, kill, or earn money dishonestly. Neither you nor your God knows the thoughts deep in my heart. Isn't your heaven meant for people like me? If your God is truly as benevolent as you claim, ought he not see the goodness in men and admit them into his realm? With all due respect comrade, your advice thus far is nonsensical rubbish.

I look forward to receiving your apology and hear no more babbling about your God's love.

Talk to you soon.
Marawi

Thursday, July 22, 1993
1517 Year Zero BCE Road
Paradise, God's Kingdom

My Dear Bother,

I trust that all is well. Thank you for asking me to offer a heavenly perspective to the points you raised.

Kneeling is not a sign of weakness but that of strength, for when a person kneels before God, it shows two things: that you acknowledge the Father's sovereignty and your freedom from sin and the power of darkness. Kneeling demonstrates freedom from the preoccupations of this present age and signals a firm "no" to the prince of the domain you abide in. Given the increasing state of depression, loneliness, and hopelessness on Planet Earth, a life of solitude that does not include leaning on God often ends up in disaster when tragedy strikes; for God is not an intangible force as you tend to think. Can one see the wind or energy? Of course not. Yet they are existing forces created by a majestic Creator whose power far exceeds that of these two elements combined. Suppose you were given a book with illustrations and were told that it fell from the sky. Would you believe it? Of course not. Any thinking person would reason that books do not write themselves, nor do images and illustrations fit themselves perfectly between words. Does a plane or robot come into existence as a result of chance from the wind gathering up metal particles in a dump site? Of course not. These two examples illustrate the absurdity of the belief that the universe self-created, without the ingenuity of a Creator behind its countless wonders. Do you honestly believe that the highly complex human DNA, the countless planets, and the intricacies of nature have no intelligent designer? Your double standard as a firm believer of science, which mainly deals with unseen things and forces, and your insistence on concrete evidence for the existence of God is troublesome.

As for your character, I applaud and commend you on doing your best not to steal, kill, or earn money dishonestly. These are indeed noble virtues for which each and every human being ought to strive. However, you erred greatly in assuming that God admits his creatures into heaven because they are good. Apostle Paul said, "Wherefore the law was our schoolmaster to bring us unto Christ, that we might be justified by faith."[13] He is saying that attempting to be good, in this case, trying to abide by the Ten Commandments, will never be sufficient to attain eternity with God. The Law was given to show man his shortcomings and need of a savior, for he cannot even keep ten laws, let alone earn his way to heaven. Humans are inherently bent toward wickedness and iniquity, and the salvation story is about undeserved grace that God gives to humans while they are still sinners. Jesus did not come and die on the cross to make bad people good, but rather so that dead people may live.[14] In fact, this is the hallmark of Christianity. Virtually all other religions claim that one's good deeds have to outweigh one's bad deeds in order to attain eternal life. The Christian God, however, is a God of love who out of affection came and died on the cross, as a loving Father, in order to reconcile his creation to himself. Why wouldn't you accept this simple, uncomplicated gift?

The Bible says your divine purpose is to "Commit thy way unto the Lord; trust also in him; and he shall bring it to pass."[15] You need not go through life trying to figure it out all on your own: allow your maker to guide you. Jesus told a story that perfectly illustrates the illusion of those who believe that they have absolute control over their lives and keep God out of their future plans. In this particular parable, there was a certain man whose harvest was ripe and plentiful. Instead of praising God and committing his plans to him, he was ungrateful and began to make independent plans. What the man did not know was that God appointed him to die that very day, leaving the fruit of his labor to be enjoyed by others who neither

13. Galatians 3:24 (KJV).
14. Leonard Ravenhill
15. Psalm 37:5 (KJV).

labored nor planned to receive the plentiful harvest.[16] I caution you not to repeat the mistake of such prideful men!

Moreover, it is evident that the world has its own way of defining success, and that definition disagrees with God's definition. According to the world, success is defined by monetary accumulation, the number of post-secondary degrees obtained, the acquisition of material, perishable commodities, or having a family. God defines success distinctly different from that of the world: purpose precedes or predates success. Purpose gave birth to all humans, for they are meant to accomplish the task they were placed on earth to do. Success then, according to God's Word, is fulfilling this purpose. The Apostle Paul spoke of various gifts (wisdom, knowledge, healing, prophecy, ability to learn languages, and so forth) from the same God for the fulfillment of his will—just like the various parts of the body (big or small) work together to make a person whole.[17] This is why many successful people—based on money, credentials, and possessions—are miserable and sometimes take their own lives, because they are not in the will of God. Before a car was made, there was a need for transportation from point A to point B. Although a knife might draw a screw into a piece of wood, it will never do so effectively and will likely end up damaged because it was not designed to be a screwdriver. Obedience is critical to discovering and fulfilling one's purpose. One must spend time with God in the reading of the Scriptures, prayer, and be filled with the Holy Ghost to know the mind of God and be strengthened to fulfill the intended purpose. Most of God's children fail to carry out their intended purpose, but it is vitally important that you know that your *professional success* as you termed it and all other successes are in God's hand. He knows the end from the beginning. He will direct your life as he sees fit, and there is nothing that can restrain him in this regard.

Last, God indeed knows the thoughts deep in your heart, and no one describes human nature better than Jesus Christ who did not downplay the gravity of sin but spoke plainly against it, and died a sinless man (the only acceptable payment for man's sin) for the redemption of man. As Creator, God knows that humans are inherently sinful and filled with evil thoughts. Lord Jesus stated, "But those things which proceed out of the mouth come forth from the heart; and they defile the man. For out of the heart proceed evil thoughts, murders, adulteries, fornications, thefts, false witness,

16. See Luke 12:16–21 (KJV).

17. I Corinthians 12: 4–11 (KJV).

blasphemies: These are the things which defile a man: but to eat with un-washen hands defileth not a man."[18] The heart of man is naturally not bent on doing good but evil; evil is deeply entrenched in the human heart and without moral guidance from God, there is no hope for you and humanity at large. How many times does a negative thought cross your mind every day? The only reason that people believe they are good and worthy of God's kingdom based on their works is because of dishonesty and their alienation from God. The closer one draws to God, the more his sins become exposed as he becomes sensitive and honest with his intents and actions—for he does not compare himself to other humans but to the blameless Christ.

May God open your eyes and help you realize your sinful, deprived life and see what he created you to accomplish on earth.

Brotherly affection,
Melchizedek

Saturday, July 31, 1993
1939 Bemba Road
Kamda, Earthly Domain

Dear Peasant,

I appreciate you taking the time to attempt to respond to my questions, though you failed miserably. You elaborated further as to why I should kneel and submit to the guidance of the entity you call God. However, my position remains unchanged and unambiguous: I am not and will not bow down to an unseen and unproven force. I refuse to get on my knees and pray to an intangible force that only manifests himself in visions and a book titled *The Holy Bible*. Kneeling is a sign of defeat and submission; there-fore, I would be lowering myself to a state of insanity and madness—hence rendering my effort to solve concrete real-life issues counterproductive as I embrace vain hope. I will, therefore, continue to seek solutions to my problems independently—not in your God. Likewise, I disagree with what you said about my so-called purpose and your definition of success. I love life and the things that it has to offer. I will continue to strive to accumulate wealth, gain renown, and acquire as much possessions as possible. I do not

18. Matthew 5:18–20 (KJV).

believe in an afterlife so this is the only life I have. It is logical, therefore, that comfort, fame, and pleasure should be my primary focus. Needless to say you demean me in your letter by essentially dismissing the fact that I am a good person and focus instead on what you refer to as my sinful nature and sinful actions. I, therefore, dismiss everything written in your fictional book. My father, friends, and children told me that I am a good person with a big heart. That is all that matter.

Throughout the course of our correspondence, you have undoubtedly dug your own grave by mentioning creation, thereby challenging the big bang theory. How can you argue against a shared consensus among educated individuals that your God does not exist, for no one can see him? I dare you to offer one counter-perspective to the big bang theory and the confusion and complexity of religion that gives birth to a variety of vain beliefs.

I expect you to respond to the questions I ask in this letter, and not waste time on nonsensical babbling.

Yours,
Marawi

~

Monday, August 9, 1993
1517 Year Zero BCE Road
Paradise, God's Kingdom

My dear Brother,

Greetings. I trust you are in perfect health and your family is doing well. To answer your inquiry concerning creation, consider the first words of *The Holy Bible*: "In the beginning God created the heaven and the earth. And the earth was without form, and void; and darkness was upon the face of the deep. And the Spirit of God moved upon the face of the waters. And God said, Let there be light: and there was light. And God saw the light, that it was good: and God divided the light from the darkness. And God called the light Day, and the darkness he called Night."[19] The big bang theory—the counter-perspective offered by nonbelievers—stipulates that the universe has a beginning and started with an explosion. This claim collaborates with

19. Genesis 1:1–5 (KJV).

the biblical account of creation because a close, objective examination of the two perspectives reveals that they do align and are not mutually exclusive, because God is the uncaused first cause and is outside of space, time, and matter. The problem is that although scientists are well aware that the world was created by God, they knowingly misguide the feeble minded— those who are deprived of the knowledge of God and a desire to know him because of their own rebellion—and perpetuate the lie that the world has no Creator and humans are mere association of atomic particles, although 1 Corinthians 15:39–49 differs. Everything that begins to exist has a cause; therefore, the universe has a cause. God did not begin to exist; he is eternal; hence, he is the instigator—the Creator of all things.

King David once said, "When I consider thy heavens, the work of thy fingers, the moon and the stars, which thou hast ordained; What is man, that thou art mindful of him? and the son of man, that thou visitest him? For thou hast made him a little lower than the angels, and hast crowned him with glory and honour. Thou madest him to have dominion over the works of thy hands; thou hast put all things under his feet."[20] This verse affords us a glimpse into the marvels of God, and shows that in spite of his grandeur, the Lord extends his amiable hands to humans, only to be rejected as the Creator of the universe, and the maker of everything therein. God by nature cannot lie and is omnipotent. There is no need for an evolution or survival of the fittest. God simply "formed man of the dust of the ground, and breathed into his nostrils the breath of life; and man became a living soul."[21] Man therefore has the breath of God, who ordained him to multiply and populate the earth. Everything God created reproduces its own kind, including man who is created in the likeness of God and carries the divine breath in him. Women never give birth to kangaroos, cows never give birth to dogs, and cats never reproduce birds, yet ungodly science claims that man came from fish and/or apes.[22] If the pseudo-scientists' assertion is true, then there should be evolving monkeys today, since there is no supreme force (law) guiding evolution that could end it at will.

Alas, man in his illusion of grandeur thinks of himself far more highly than he truly is. The universe contains millions of galaxies and billions of stars and planets. One of the galaxies created by God Almighty is called Milky Way, within which your star is called Sun. Rotating around the sun

20. Psalms 8: 3–6 (KJV).
21. See Genesis 2:7.
22. See Genesis 1:25.

is your planet (one of the nine), Earth. In the Earth are continents. Within the continents, countries; within countries, regions; within regions, communities; within communities, neighborhoods; within neighborhoods, buildings, where finite men such as Darwin and Hawking believe their knowledge surpasses that of God. In the universe, man is not even as big as a grain of sand on the beach, and it is only by the grace of God that he is even relevant. Desist from making the blunder of prideful men who seek to erase every trace of God's fingerprint in creation and mankind.

The theory of evolution has many flaws, since anatomy and every discipline of science have thus far failed to provide a logical and acceptable explanation as to how human beings can possibly be created without God and function without their Creator. Machines are created by man but can never effectively function independently as man. The human body yields clues about the mysteries of the Creator. It is a beautiful testimony of a personable (relational) maker and speaks of the intimacy of the Lord. In philosophy, there are two opposing and contradicting positions that compete when it comes to the uniqueness of man vis-à-vis other created things and beings: materialism and immaterialism. The materialist's position revolves around matter and the functions of matter. Those who subscribe to this belief claim that there is virtually no difference between human beings and animals, and they seek to explain the origin of humans, their metaphysical attributes, and distinctive personalities through the theory of evolution. The immaterialists hold that matter and its functions are necessary but not sufficient to explain human uniqueness, thus making the existence of the greatest and most supreme power in the universe possible. An objective comparison of these two paradigms will lead an honest seeker of truth to conclude that the immaterialists have a stronger case because humans are indeed distinct from every other form of matter. Furthermore, the concepts of justice, equality, and human rights that most unbelievers claim to stand for, collapse in a materialistic and atheistic paradigm—they are only possible in immaterialism and theism; for in materialism and by extension atheism, there is no rational argument against mass atrocities such as genocide, oppression, abortion, and war crimes. Humans are merely replaceable and recyclable commodities, good for a season and with no intrinsic value. This degrading view is designed to tarnish the image of God's golden and prized creatures: humans.

Your arrogance hinders you from pondering the possibility of a personal Creator. If you indeed place your faith in the big bang theory, there are a number of questions you ought to ask yourself: What was the force behind the explosion? Was it created or uncreated? After the explosion, what determined that particles come together perfectly to form the planets, stars, and galaxies? What keeps the universe in a constant and flawless state of existence? What guarantees that the sun will rise tomorrow and the earth will rotate perfectly on its axis? Since atheists cannot provide a coherent response to these lingering questions, they perpetuate the notion that whatever created the universe must itself be uncreated, eternal, and allpowerful; thereby affirming the fact that these are the characteristics of the Christian God, for Christians hold that God is uncreated, omnipotent, omnipresent, and omniscient. YHWH (the Hebrew name of God) repeatedly stated his name—I Am.[23] He was, he is, and he shall always be.

Your pride makes you claim that you are created in the image of nothing. Indeed, evolution and naturalism hold that humans evolved from a prototype—be it primate-looking, aquatic, terrestrial, or extraterrestrial. It is a monumental blunder to assume that by subscribing to a certain scientific belief, one is exempt from criticism, for deceptive science—atheism—in itself is a religion and belief system. Your society trains people to mock Christianity and have no interest in examining the Bible to draw their own conclusion. When I lived on Earth, I was confident that I would never have to deal with God, even if he was real. Accordingly, I lived a careless life; emboldened by a false sense of empowerment and grandeur that pseudoscience offered me. I used the malevolent argument of God and evil to draw many people, including Christians, away from following Christ, and I repeatedly neglected the call to turn to the Creator, including pleas from my close friends and family members. You are a victim of the same system, and I warn you against giving in to such lies.

I wish you well.
Melchizedek

---

23. See Exodus 3:14.

3

What is the Path to Truth?

Saturday, September 11, 1993
1939 Bemba Road
Kamda, Earthly Domain

Dear friend,

I had the delight of reading your letter. It was quite amusing and frankly some of the things you made mention of and the claims that you advanced are quite fanatical to say the least. Indeed, you went at a great length to offer counterarguments to the widely accepted theory of evolution. Although this theory has nothing to do with your God, I am surprised at how far you went to align it with your theistic preconceptions. Although unconvinced, I admit that some of your questions are thought-provoking. I always assumed that only those who place their faith in the imaginary God hold a paradigm with weak points. However, you challenged me to put more time into studying the theory of evolution to show you that creation does not necessitate the existence of your God.

You invoked the position of the materialists and immaterialist to support your view concerning the existence of God. This is a flawed argument because most scientists subscribe to the position of the materialists. We are, indeed, mere physical matter with no value after life, let alone intrinsic value. As far as I am concerned, only physical life has been concretely observed, and no one besides the myth of Jesus of Nazareth died and came back to life. We can, therefore, conclude that man is composed of particles that disintegrate and return to nature upon death.

In light of your claim that there exists a singular God, whose god is the true one? The Greeks'? The Romans'? The Animists'? The Muslims', Buddhists', Hindus'? Indeed, Christianity and its view of God appear to be a morphing of Egyptian mythology and other faiths in the Near East. Mr. Melchizedek, rest assured that the concept of God is a novel invention advanced to control a certain group of gullible people, and religion is nothing but a social construct that varies from one culture to another.

I believe there is no escape route for you, because if you admit that all the various gods represent your God then there would certainly be a logical inconsistency in your assumption. On the other hand, if you claim that all these gods are false then you must explain why this is so.

Salutations.
Marawi

～

Sunday, October 17, 1993
1517 Year Zero BCE Road
Paradise, God's Kingdom

Bonjour mon frère,

May the God who created all things continue to bless our friendship, which extends beyond the grave, and erase the lies of the big bang theory from your mind and shower you with his incomparable love. Thank you for your partial, though unintentional, admission that Jesus Christ is the only person who died and lives again, for I serve a living Savior!

Contrary to the prevalent misconception held by many people, the concept of the greatest, supreme entity precedes the Judeo-Christian era (though the lost did not follow his command to worship the Creator and not the creation). The diverse societies that preceded Abraham neglected this knowledge, and various societies in Africa, the Americas, Europe, and Oceania hold a distorted belief. Since mankind rejected God even after the great flood, rebelled against him by refusing to scatter throughout the earth, and revolted under the leadership of Nimrod and attempted to reach the Almighty in heaven by building the infamous Tower of Babel, man brought confusion upon himself as he lost fellowship with his Creator. The Lord in his divine grace and mercy, however, had a plan of salvation and redemption for man: God would choose a humble man (Abraham) and later a seemingly insignificant nation (Israel) to offer man a chance to reconcile with him and restore the lost fellowship. For the Jews, the decisive moment that marked the revelation and authenticity of God occurred when YHWH revealed himself to Abram in Ur of the Chaldeans and promised to make his posterity thriving, dominant, and glorious, if they would keep his commandments. Hundreds of years before the advent of the Jewish nation, typically referred to as Israel, God foretold the slavery that the Israelites would be subjected to in Egypt and their subsequent deliverance when he told Abraham "Know of a surety that thy seed shall be a stranger in a land that is not theirs, and shall serve them; and they shall afflict them four hundred years; And also that nation, whom they shall serve, will I judge: and afterward shall they come out with great substance."[1] The Lord also told Abram that he would no longer be referred to as such, but would be called Abraham, for he made him a father of many nations. Likewise, the name Israel was first used by the Lord as he spoke with Jacob (Abraham's grandson) and made a covenant with him: "And he said, Thy name shall be called no more Jacob, but Israel . . ."[2] Last, the Almighty also foretold the coming of universal salvation from the Jewish nation when the he spoke to Isaac (Jacob's father): "And I will make thy seed to multiply as the stars of heaven, and will give unto thy seed all these countries; and in thy seed shall all the nations of the earth be blessed; Because Abraham obeyed my voice, and kept my charge, my commandments, my statutes, and my laws."[3]

Christianity is a product of Judaism and began with the arrival of Jesus Christ, its central figure. From its inception, Christianity faced opposition, most notably from the Jewish ruling aristocracy, the Roman Empire, and unbelieving gentiles (non-Jews). Emboldened by the resurrection of Jesus Christ and the promise of eternal life, Christians frequently chose martyrdom with unwavering faith rather than surrendering their beliefs; many were mercilessly tortured and murdered under Roman emperors such as Nero and Diocletian. The initial believers were so devoted and determined to spread the teachings of Jesus Christ with such resolve and zeal that they increasingly gained converts among the Roman working class as well as

1. Genesis 15: 13–14 (KJV).
2. Genesis 32:28 (KJV).
3. Genesis 26: 4–5 (KJV).

the nobility. Thanks to their sacrifice, initiated of course by the Lord Jesus Christ and other believers such as Apostle Paul—a zealous member of the Pharisees (a group of well-versed experts in Judaism), who ironically converted to Christianity on his way to Damascus to persecute Christians—that modern Christians have the chance to freely experience the wonders of the Creator. Alas, presently on earth, the Word of God is profaned, his name blasphemed, and his existence mocked. The existence and credibility of the Almighty are questioned through pseudoscience and technology, but nothing can erase the fingerprints of God in nature and in the lives of those who choose to know him.

In regard to your reiteration that Christianity is a counterfeit of Egyptian mythology, and that religion at its core is a social construct to reinforce morality, dear friend, I encourage you to do a personal comparative study between the Bible and the myths that you are equating it to. The Bible is a historical book (it can be archeologically and historically verified) and contains elements of the supernatural (also called miracles) that are reliable. From prophecies regarding the formation and destruction of many great empires such as Assyria, Babylon, and Persia, to the prediction of the advent of the Roman Empire and the life and death of Jesus Christ, there are no scientific explanations for the numerous events that occurred in a precise manner as the Bible predicted hundreds of years beforehand, other than an all-knowing God who knows the end from the beginning. Read the book of Daniel, chapter seven to chapter twelve, and see the fingerprint of the supernatural in predicting events that were centuries away from the time of the writing of this book. Due to your insistence on the supremacy of science, consider the following scientific facts recorded in the Bible, hundreds of years before science: The Earth's free float in space[4], the life of the flesh in the blood[5], and the Circle of the Earth[6].

Further, the Bible is unique in its origin, its content, and its preservation through the ages; it is a book of revelation. Nonbiblical books simply record truths discovered by man through observation, but the Bible unveils spiritual truth that man could otherwise not know. When one purchases a book, its author may be dead or distant from the buyer and reader. The Bible, however, is the only book that comes with its author (God) who speaks directly to the seeker of truth, regardless of location and time of life.

---

4. See Job 26:7

5. See Leviticus 17: 11

6 See Isaiah 40: 22

It's a book that does not grow old and from which thousands of sermons have been preached; it's the most suppressed book through the ages, yet the most sought after and most revolutionary in the history of man—not just spiritually but in the development of law, science, education, and health. Moreover, the myths that you are comparing Christianity to are just myths, as you stated. There is no verifiable evidence that shows Zeus or any of the other gods made contact with mankind. The Bible, on the other hand, has settings and personalities associated with it that can be independently verified apart from Jesus Christ. Further, the concept of one God, with no co-equal gods and goddesses is exclusively a Judeo-Christian concept. It's true that various cultures since the dawn of time have the notion of a supreme deity, but they are always associated with lesser or equal deities. Be mindful that you are speaking of a belief whose chief character boldly told the Pharisees and Scribes, "For as Jonas was three days and three nights in the whale's belly; so shall the Son of man be three days and three nights in the heart of the earth,"[7] and then rose three days after his crucifixion, proving that he is no charlatan.

What you refer to as religion, though in its modern context is more organized and centralized, does not warrant the term *social construct*. Any honest person would say that the desire to seek a higher power is innate in them and the longing for transcendent communion is real. This is equally true for those who claim to have no ties to belief in a particular religion, although they prefer to reject this fact when push comes to shove. My dear friend, God did not just create us, but he instilled in us the desire to know him, regardless of our location and upbringing. Notwithstanding that various groups of people worshipped various deities, most cultures before the contemporary era, however, believed in the concept of a supreme God (although they also gave the title to false gods). In Greece it was Zeus, who, ironically according to his venerators, did not create the cosmos; in Ancient Egypt, Amun-Ra; Su in the N'gambay tradition in southern Chad; Shiva in Hinduism; or the Ahura Mazda of the Babylonians. Many of these false gods are the same but only change name from one society to another. An obvious partiality on the side of critics is that an immense expectation and criticism is directed at Christians and their God, without realizing that most cultures that predated Christianity and those that still exist today, have their own distorted paradigm as to how the world came to be. These paradigms are blatantly fake and unrealistic, and the only reason they

7. Matthew 12:40 (KJV).

haven't been criticized is for the profit of those who seek to perpetuate the notion that Christianity is the problem and the enemy; therefore anything associated with Christianity needs to be eradicated.

The Christian God, I must stress, is unique: he is One in three persons, he came and died on the cross for his creation, and he is a forgiving Father who accepts his children into his domain because of grace, not works. Moreover, your argument that religion is a social construct does not stand against criticism because isolated, socially distinct cultures tend to have a common denominator and belief: the existence of a being worthy of worship. This reality further attests to the significance of religion beyond its perceived social causes and the burning desire of man to find his Creator. In Christianity, however, the emphasis is put on relationship (with God) rather than religion, because religion is often associated with rituals and man's attempt to earn his way to heaven rather than getting there through unmerited grace.

My dear brother, the Armenians say, "By talking too much, a man's voice turns into the voice of the tree." Accordingly, I choose to end my letter now.

I expect your reply in the near future.

Your Faithful Brother,
Melchizedek

4

Pain and Suffering

Thursday, November 11, 1993
1939 Bemba Road
Kamda, Earthly Domain

Good Evening, Melchizedek.

I disagree with much of what you shared in your last letter. Indeed, everything you wrote comes from a narrow perspective, marred by the image of the entity you call God. Your pathetic attempt to give merit to the misconception of a singular force in the universe is amusing. Your attempt also at discrediting the big bang theory is an utter failure. It seems that you are clueless about science, and you should keep silent on matters you know nothing about. You challenged the sacred big bang theory by claiming it did not come out of nothing but had an intelligent mind behind it. Let me inform you that if such a being exists, he is certainly imperfect because there is no rationale for the diseases, suffering, death, hunger, murder, and oppression that humans go through. Should I grant you the benefit of the doubt, your God is still not allpowerful as you portray him to be because of the presence of evil in the world. I, as an atheist and human being, can do a much better job than your God. We here in the West are taught from a young age that science (verifiable) trumps and supersedes myths about a certain Creator and the illusion of religion.

Further, your claim that God revealed himself to every culture is not valid and bears little credibility. There is no way he has done so in the past, and he has not done it at the present in my opinion. I also vehemently reject the idea that your God is unique and remain steadfast in my conviction that all religions came about as a product of social construct. During antiquity, science and other empirical subjects were not advanced. Therefore, every time a phenomenon occurred that can easily be explained today, people invoked the notion of a singular, unique God to explain the seemingly unexplainable. For example, when it rained, many ancient societies referred to the god of rain as the one who opened the gates of heaven to let water out.

I shared your notes with my dear wife Dina and my children, and we are all entertained by your ridiculous arguments. Having said that, though the life of Paul gained our interest, we look forward to hearing more fantasies from you and mocking your nonsensical assumptions about your God and the great subject of science. People such as you are the reason why we in the West are taught from a young age to despise religion and to elevate secular values above dangerous faiths such as Christianity. I am particularly curious what you will say now about the existence of diverse evil and suffering in the world.

Open your mind and stop being so stupid and close-minded!

Till next time,
Marawi Njerabé

Saturday, December 4, 1993
1517 Year Zero BCE Road
Paradise, God's Kingdom

My dear Brother,

I appreciate the time you take to write me back. Remember, the point of our correspondence is to discuss what truth is, not to attack one another on a personal level with disrespect and hurtful words.

It is indeed interesting that you did not investigate the points I raised but simply dismissed them as nonsensical, and reject God without giving him a fair hearing. Concerning general revelation, I choose to let the Bible speak for itself. Read Romans 1: 18–32 and let me know. You assumed that there is no rebuttal to your statement directed at the Almighty: "there is no rationale for the diseases, suffering, death, hunger, murder, and oppression that humans go through." My dear brother Marawi, evil is not a thing in itself, nor has it come from the Creator: evil is a result of disorder in the creational will—a consequence of God's absence and man's separateness from God (the first sin). The question ought to be why good things happen on an Earth inhabited by vile men with wicked hearts who have no regard for a holy and just God. If the Lord were to make your planet crystal clear again, it would be polluted the next day because of man's wicked heart.[1] It is regrettable that man fails to consider that some of the evil and suffering he faces: AIDS, COVID-19, famine, genocide . . . could and are sometimes engineered by man for sinister reasons, for self-interest and in the grand scheme of things: satanic influence to advance the kingdom of darkness. God gets all the blame and the other possibility is neglected. You are also invoking moral objectivity to pose the question; otherwise it would be meaningless, had there been no God. In posing this particular question, which happens to be the primary objection and argument against the existence of the Lord, you tacitly assume that there is such thing as good and evil. If you assume, therefore, that there is such a thing as good, you also thereby concede that there is such a thing as evil. If good and evil are objectively true, then it follows logically that there must be an objective moral law on the basis of which you can differentiate between good and evil. If there is a moral law, there must be a moral law giver, for if there is no moral law giver, there is no objective morality. If there is no objective morality, there is no such thing as good and evil, for it becomes a matter of subjectivity. Your question then, self-destructs and crumbles in an atheistic framework.[2]

Dear friend, as you can see, apart from the Christian notion of a supreme God, your question is meaningless because evolution and natural selection only deal with the survival of the fittest and what it takes for humans to adapt to their changing environment. Once you bring God into the picture, however, your question becomes more meaningful. In illustrating and addressing the question of good and evil, consider the following parable: A certain young man used to criticize and blame God for everything bad that happened. Prior to death, he would attribute anything good or positive to mother nature and the exploits of man, for example, provision, health, prosperity, and longevity. Although he did not believe in God, he would blame everything bad or negative on God, such as earthquakes, maladies, famine, rape, poverty, and death. For this young man, the God of the

1. Paul Washer
2. Ravi Zacharias

33

Christians is good for nothing but is the author of the misery and suffering of his creation. He thus erred and led many people astray. He lived to be an old man, and there came a day when he finally died. Shortly thereafter he stood before God for the final judgment, since the man had never taken the time to receive Jesus Christ in his heart. Notwithstanding his obvious guilt, he had the audacity to point his finger at God and say, "I never believed in your name, nor considered in the slightest bit that I would stand before you to be judged. Tell me one thing before I face eternal damnation: If you are a holy and just God, why haven't you sent the cure for cancer, HIV⁄AIDS, and the bubonic plague that has devastated societies and decimated the human population over the centuries?" A voice replied, "Aren't you an avid supporter of the pro-choice movement?" To which the man responded, "Yes, indeed." The voice responded, "God has sent you his angels, indeed, millions of highly intelligent experts to solve your plights and struggles with diseases, inequality, and various social problems. You have, however, murdered them all before they were ever born." The man looked at God and said, "I never looked at it from this perspective, but I beg your forgiveness. Is there one more room in your heaven for me?" To which the reply was, "God has done all he could to invite you to be with him, but you were too busy glorifying yourself all your life. Since he is a just God, he must render justice and let you go and commune with the devil—the one you made the master of your life." The newly deceased man then asked to come back to life to warn his loved ones that were making the same mistake, but the voice replied, "Man's heart is so hardened that they reject my one and only begotten Son; there is no way they would listen to you."[3]

In dealing with the problem of evil and suffering, we can imagine four possible scenarios when God created the universe, the earth, and mankind. He can create (1) nothing (you and I wouldn't be here today to carry on this correspondence); (2) a world where there is only good and in which there is no free will or love because humans have to be mere robots that are programmed to only do good; (3) a world where only evil exists (an immoral world), which if history repeats itself, would eventually self-destruct; or (4) a world such as the present one, where evil and good exist—where virtue and vice coexist.[4] As you shall come to realize upon reflection, the only model where freewill and love could exist is the last one, the world you live in today.

3. See Luke 16: 19–31.
4. Ravi Zacharias

On a different note, I am glad that the life of Apostle Paul (formerly Saul of Tarsus) gained your interest. Sometimes I compare your life and mine to that of Paul. Indeed, prior to my conversion, I was a passionate and fervent opponent of Christianity, and although I did not actively persecute Christians, I mocked them and wished evil upon them. Like Paul, it took a major incident (my parents' passing on the way to the Republic of Chad) for me to come to the cross and ask the Lord Jesus Christ into my heart. Likewise, my brother, you are like Saul—the pre-Christian version of Paul of Tarsus—at the moment: You have an ardent zeal and loyalty to a belief that deviates from the gospel; you have a great deal of contempt for Christians and remain stiff-necked in spite of overwhelming evidence that Jesus Christ is the only way to God the Father. I am, however, convinced that like Paul and like me, God will soften your heart and you shall come to know the love of Jesus Christ—at his appointed time and divine will.

'Tis regrettable that children in your world are taught from infancy that science is paramount, and secular, liberal values trump Christian values. In doing so, your society disregards the God who foresaw humanity's problems and gave guidelines to avoid them. For instance, God said, "And if a man entice a maid that is not betrothed, and lie with her, he shall surely endow her to be his wife."[5] If heeded, this command would save modern man from the ever-worsening problem of fatherlessness and the upbringing of children by one parent; it would ensure the education of children by both parents. To avoid the oppression of the weak, he instructed, "Thou shalt neither vex a stranger, nor oppress him: for ye were strangers in the land of Egypt;"[6] "Also thou shalt not oppress a stranger: for ye know the heart of a stranger, seeing ye were strangers in the land of Egypt."[7] "Ye shall not afflict any widow, or fatherless child. If thou afflict them in any wise, and they cry at all unto me, I will surely hear their cry."[8] To discourage usury and dishonesty in financial dealings, he declared, "If thou lend money to any of my people that is poor by thee, thou shalt not be to him as an usurer, neither shalt thou lay upon him usury."[9] To combat the spread of sexually transmitted diseases, God repeatedly condemned fornication (sex

5. Exodus 22: 16 (KJV).
6. Exodus 22:21 (KJV).
7. Exodus 23:9 (KJV).
8. Exodus 22:22 (KJV).
9. Exodus 22: 25 (KJV).

before marriage) and adultery (extramarital affair) both in the Old Testament and New Testament.

I am thrilled to hear that your wife and children are also interested in finding truth. God will not turn away those who diligently and sincerely seek him; therefore, inform your wife and children to ask any questions they would like, and that there is always one more room in heaven for a new believer.

May the peace of God rest upon your family.

Your brother,
Melchizedek

Saturday, December 18, 1993
1939 Bemba Road
Kamda, Earthly Domain

Melchizedek,

I unapologetically demand that you stop being stupid and become open-minded. As your friend, I feel obliged to tell you that and sometimes tough love is necessary in dealing with a bigot like you. I started this correspondence with the intention of discovering truth but you start to irritate me by basing all your assumptions on the Christian paradigm—you grind my gears, man. As for the points you raised about why your God permits evil in the world, I choose to not contemplate them because there is simply too much evil in this world to imagine that a good, honorable God has a purpose for it all.

To your credit though, I must confess that you raised a thought-provoking point when you explained the options available to your God, and the various scenarios he could come up with. I reject the idea that good and evil result from freewill, but you made a sound argument that merits consideration.

Please do not get your hopes up. Just because I stated that the life of Paul gained my interest does not mean you should jump to conclusions, assuming that I am ready to accept your imaginary God. Friend, you ought not to delight in the fact that you have committed an intellectual suicide by becoming a Christian. Indeed, I knew you before and after you conversion so I can tell you with unerring certainly how foolish your decision was: you went from an articulate and charismatic opponent of Christianity to a man who merely believes in a Maker and a book title *The Holy Bible*. I, therefore, insist that you do not compare me to the backward first century illiterate man you call Paul. I am from the civilized West and am intelligent enough not to become a Christian—comparing my life to that of Paul is like comparing apples to oranges. You one the other hand, can compare your foolish decision to convert to Christianity to that of Paul.

How dare you question the supremacy of pragmatism and secularism? Our society owes its success and prosperity to these two ideals, and we proudly raise the future generation to champion them and forsake the old way of religion. The fact that you cited some examples from the Bible to support your point certainty does not help. My wife and children are certainly not interested in your nonsensical teachings but take pleasure in mocking you as well. So do not be so ignorant as to assume that they are interested in fantasies about your God.

I would like to end my letter by asking for further clarification regarding the question of evil and challenge you about the following: Given that you offered a lame counterperspective as to why evil exists in the world, is there a difference between a Christians and non-Christians facing suffering and challenges in life?

Yours,
Marawi

Tuesday, January 4, 1994
1517 Year Zero BCE Road
Paradise, God's Kingdom

Lalé Marawi,

Apostle Paul is not the man you paint him to be and by your standards, he was far more educated than you. Among his many credentials, he was a Pharisee.[10] His conversion is radical (he went from the persecutor of the Church to a believer) and you should not dismiss the transformational experience he had on the way to Damascus.

10. See Philippians 3: 5–6; Acts 23: 6; Acts 9

Believers (Christians) are not exempted from pain and suffering, contrary to the prevalent and widespread prosperity gospel. Comfort, wealth, and physical wellness are never promised to followers of Christ in their earthly life; these are blessings and privileges, not entitlements. Christians are commanded to set their affections on things in God's kingdom and strive to be Christlike. The Lord warned his followers of tribulations to come due to their faith in God: "Think not that I am come to send peace on earth: I came not to send peace, but a sword. For I am come to set a man at variance against his father, and the daughter against her mother, and the daughter in law against her mother in law. And a man's foes shall be they of his own household. He that loveth father or mother more than me is not worthy of me: and he that loveth son or daughter more than me is not worthy of me."[11] Suffering was not a part of the Lord's plan because as a loving Father, God purposed for man to live eternally in peace; however, due to Adam's sin in the garden of Eden, man—not the Lord—brought sin and death upon himself. Furthermore, God wants his creation to voluntarily (free will) worship him for his magnificence—not out of fear of retribution or because of a promise to live comfortably on earth. Suffering, though often regarded as a bad thing, does indeed have positive sides. Just like a child learns not to touch fire by actually touching it and feeling pain, suffering serves as a constant reminder that humans are not complete and need empowerment from a higher power to overcome the challenges of life. In my personal life, I would have never accepted Jesus Christ, the Son of God, into my heart and lived for God had it not been for the tragic and painful loss of my parents in that infamous voyage to Chad. If God is taken out of the equation, the question becomes even more meaningless and incomprehensible; for evolution and naturalism deal with existence and survival, not morality—they offer no comfort in the time of storm. It is evident that there is no hope, comfort, and justice in the theory of evolution since it solely encourages self-preservation and holds that upon death, each organism turns into an inactive material, with no hope of life beyond the grave; thus Pablo Escobar and David Livingston face the same fate; Leopold II of Belgium and missionary Mary Baker face the same fate: eternal oblivion. Evolution is, therefore, a degrading theory that robs humanity of its value, and fails miserably vis-à-vis metaphysics and ethics.

Further, the second chapter of Genesis vividly illustrates the question of evil and suffering: "And the Lord commanded the man, saying, of every

11. Matthew 10: 34–37 (KJV).

tree of the garden thou mayest freely eat: But of the tree of knowledge of good and evil, thou shalt not eat of it: for in the day thou eatest thereof thou shalt surely die." This passage, in essence, says the following: Do not play God, for the day you play God, your doom shall commence. As an all-knowing Father, the Lord knows that when humans are given the option between good and evil, virtue and vice, their heart is always inclined to the latter; he therefore created a way of escape (through his only begotten Son). Evil is brought upon the world and humanity as a product of man's sin, yet God takes all the blame. Nonetheless, there is a comforting promise in the Beatitudes, offered by the Lord Jesus Christ in the Sermon on the Mount to believers:

> Blessed are the poor in spirit; for theirs is the kingdom of heaven.
> Blessed are they that mourn: for they shall be comforted.
> Blessed are the meek: for they shall inherit the earth.
> Blessed are they which do hunger and thirst after righteousness: for they shall be filled.
> Blessed are the merciful: for they shall obtain mercy.
> Blessed are the pure in heart: for they shall see God.
> Blessed are the peacemakers: for they shall be called the children of God.
> Blessed are they which are persecuted for righteousness' sake: for theirs is the kingdom of heaven.
> Blessed are ye, when men shall revile you, and persecute you, and shall say all manner of evil against you falsely, for my sake.
> Rejoice, and be exceeding glad: for great is your reward in heaven: for so persecuted they the prophets which were before you.[12]

To gain an insight into the mind of a true believer when confronted with the idea of evil and suffering, examine the following words penned by the Apostle Paul in his letter to the Romans:

> "What shall we then say to these things? If God be for us, who can be against us? He that spared not his own Son, but delivered him up for us all, how shall he not with him also freely give us all things? Who shall lay any thing to the charge of God's elect? It is God that justifieth. Who is he that condemneth? It is Christ that died, yea rather, that is risen again, who is even at the right hand of God, who also maketh intercession for us. Who shall separate us from the love of Christ? shall tribulation, or distress, or persecution, or famine, or nakedness, or peril, or sword? As it is written, For thy sake we are killed all the day long; we are accounted as

---

12. Matthew 5: 3–12 (KJV).

sheep for the slaughter. Nay, in all these things we are more than conquerors through him that loved us. For I am persuaded, that neither death, nor life, nor angels, nor principalities, nor powers, nor things present, nor things to come, Nor height, nor depth, nor any other creature, shall be able to separate us from the love of God, which is in Christ Jesus our Lord."[13]

It is a grave mistake to assume that Christians and their God have no solace or answer when the question "Why is there so much evil in the world?" is asked. It is also naive to think that Christianity offers no solution to the diverse plights of man, for once God is kept in the paradigm, the question of suffering and its remedies become all the more clear and sensical. Believers are aware that the domain they live in (Planet Earth) is ruled by darkness. They are, therefore, not permanent residents there, but foreigners on their way to a glorified eternity, as promised "And God shall wipe away all tears from their eyes; and there shall be no more death, neither sorrow, nor crying, neither shall there be any more pain: for the former things are passed away. And he that sat upon the throne said, Behold, I make all things new."[14]

I trust you will look at the question of suffering from a new perspective and light.

Cordially,
Melchizedek

13. Romans 8:31–39 (KJV).
14. Revelation 21: 4–5 (KJV).

5

Who is Jesus Christ?

Monday, January 17, 1994
1939 Bemba Road
Kamda, Earthly Domain

Dear confused and misguided friend.

I have thoroughly read your letter but do not have the time to offer rebuttals to your babbling concerning what is the difference between a non-Christian and the so-called believer when they face suffering and the challenges of life. As a highly successful employee, I choose not to waste my time on nonsense, but will rather bring a new topic to our discussion: Who is Jesus Christ? Who gave him that title? If you are implying that he has a special status among men by referring to him as the Son of God, you have surely erred, my friend. No doubt Jesus Christ appears to be another invented character to render your myth about God more appealing. If your God truly exists, why would he need to have a son through whom mankind can receive forgiveness?

I am well aware of the fairytale in the garden of Eden that is frequently narrated to justify the presence of evil in this world. Once again, I categorically reject the notion that a certain God created humans in his image. Also, as a proud supporter of the feminist movement, I am deeply offended by the tale of Adam and Eve in the garden of Eden. It is a fabricated farce meant to belittle women and make them look perpetually evil in the eyes of man. No person in their right state of mind would believe that a certain woman named Eve was the first perpetrator of evil on Planet Earth, through the consumption of "the forbidden fruit."

Additionally, what's the point of following your God if he does not promise financial stability, emotional comfort, and physical tranquility? Contrary to the wealth and intellect that civilized individuals enjoy, you assert that by surrendering one's life to Jesus Christ, an individual is putting himself at further risk because all hell will break loose and target him. Jesus, you claim, promised his disciples that their parents, brethren, and friends, will turn against them. Why in the world did they become Christians when they knew with certainty that their socioeconomic situation will be greatly disturbed? In my highly esteemed opinion, Christians have made a foolish decision that I, as a rational and educated person, will never make. I am content with making moral decisions and judgment based on my atheistic and scientific beliefs. As a reminder, I deem myself more moral than your God.

Last, I would like to inform you that you have become a subject of scorn, not just at our house but also beyond. My capable children shared your notes with their teachers and friends, and they collectively agree that you have a serious mental problem that needs to be taken care of. My wife also spoke to her friends concerning you and there is a consensus among them that you need to be readmitted back to Planet Earth so that you can regain your sanity and be exposed to reality.

Take care!
Marawi

∼

Wednesday, February 2, 1994
1517 Year Zero BCE Road
Paradise, God's Kingdom

My dear friend,

I rejoice that I am counted worthy to suffer for Christ's sake and delight in being the subject of your scorn for God's sake. I consider these acts as a reminder that I am sharing truth about God, and since the natural (unsaved) man hates God, it is inevitable that he will oppose those who take a stand for him. Your attack on the only begotten Son of God is born out of willful ignorance (intentional contempt for his name). The Bible says

"For there are three that bear record in heaven, the Father, the Word, and the Holy Ghost: and these three are one."[1] The Word is who you question. Christ Jesus is unarguably the most known personality in the history of mankind. Today, there are over 2 billion Christians (although some are nominal) who are a direct product of his teachings while he lived in modern Israel, between 1 BC and 32 AD. The Gregorian calendar, modern day medicine, and the concepts of university, law, justice, human rights, and social structure are deeply indebted to Jesus Christ. He preached against much of the contemporary plights of society: injustice, oppression, segregation, suffering, social hierarchy, and murder. As theologian Philip Schaff beautifully puts it:

> "Jesus of Nazareth, without money and arms, conquered more millions than Alexander the Great, Caesar, Mohammed, and Napoleon; without science and learning, he shed more light on things human and divine than all philosophers and scholars combined; without the eloquence of school, he spoke such words of life as were never spoken before or since, and produced effects which lie beyond the reach of orator or poet; without writing a single line, he set more pens in motion, and furnished themes for more sermons, orations, discussions, learned volumes, works of art, and songs of praise than the whole army of great men of ancient and modern times. As the centuries pass, the evidence is accumulating that, measured by his effect on history, Jesus is the most influential life ever lived on this planet. Socrates taught for 40 years, Plato for 50, Aristotle for 40, and Jesus for only 3. Yet the influence of Christ's 3-year ministry infinitely transcends the impact left by the combined 130 years of teaching from these men who were among the greatest philosophers of all antiquity."

Moreover, Christ did not witness of himself. His disciples, secular scholars, the Jewish aristocracy, and Roman historians wrote about his miracles and his impeccable character. John, one of Jesus' disciples (an eyewitness) began his first letter thus:

> That which was from the beginning, which we have heard, which we have seen with our eyes, which we have looked upon, and our hands have handled, of the Word of life; (For the life was manifested, and we had seen it, and bear witness, and shew unto you that eternal life, which was with the Father, and was manifested unto us;) That which we have seen and heard declare we unto you,

1. I John 5: 7 (KJV).

43

that ye also may have fellowship with us: and truly our fellowship is with the Father, and with his Son Jesus Christ. And these things write we unto you, that your joy may be full. This then is the message which we have heard of him, and declare unto you, that God is light, and in him is no darkness at all.[2]

This primary source document irrefutably proves the existence of Jesus Christ and his ministry in Judaea–Samaria, along with Apostles James and Jude who were brothers of Christ and wrote epistles in the New Testament called the Book of James and Jude, respectively. Apostle John repeatedly uses the words *heard* and *seen* in his letter, implying that he was not only Jesus' disciple but witnessed his awesome wonders and teachings. Paul in his epistle to the Corinthians made mention of those who have seen Jesus Christ after his resurrection and were still alive, as if to say if you do not believe me, go ask them.[3] In addition, the coming of Jesus Christ was prophesied centuries earlier by several prophets, most notably, Elijah, Isaiah, Jeremiah, and Daniel. There are over 300 prophesies about Jesus Christ in the Old Testament. God and his angels bear witness to him as well. I would encourage you to examine Isaiah 53 and see if the prophecies therein are of human origin. Jesus' name and divinity are not self-arrogated, nor an illusion of grandeur. He is no imaginary character, nor is God a myth. Arrogance brought about the downfall of Pharaoh, king of Egypt when he declared, "Who is the LORD, that I should obey his voice to let Israel go? I know not the LORD, neither will I let Israel go."[4]

In regard to your inquiry—"If your God truly exists, why would he need to have a Son through whom mankind can receive forgiveness?"—I am exceeding glad you enquired of the Lord. It is indeed your confusion of the nature of God that made you demean the essential role of Jesus Christ. For God to relate to us as a Father, it is critical that he directly relates to his creation. Since God is omnipotent, he could have chosen a different avenue for salvation or left man in his deprived state with no hope. Because of his immense and unlimited love for humans, however, the Lord chose to come and suffer for his creation to bring about salvation and reconciliation—since a sinful man cannot offer a satisfactory atonement for his sin. Psalm 85:10 speaks of the greatest council (meeting) that ever took place in eternity past between mercy (the Father God), truth (Jesus Christ); righteousness

2. I John 1: 1–5 (KJV).

3. See I Corinthians 15: 3–8

4. Exodus 5:2 (KJV)

(God) and peace (Jesus Christ). The Holy Spirit was present at the meeting taking note, and God in his foreknowledge affirmed that man will choose evil and sin; therefore, the Son (Jesus Christ) would come and lay down his life to redeem man. A just and equitable God requires justice for the sins and offenses of men. Therefore, Jehovah put all of man's sin and his wrath upon his Son Jesus Christ who knew no sin, so you and I do not have to face his wrath and judgment, and receive free admittance to heaven, upon accepting his Son's death on the cross as the only avenue to the Father.[5]

Dear friend, before making such a bold and fact-lacking claim concerning God being an anti-feminist, you should carefully examine the story of creation and the life of Jesus Christ who unarguably championed all rights, including for women. God is an egalitarian Creator who went as far as taking Adam's rib to make Eve. This fact is no coincidence and is significant in many ways when dealing with controversies concerning gender, for it reflects God's nature. The Lord could, for example, make Eve out of dust as he had done previously with Adam. However, he chose to take a part of man to make a woman.[6]

A woman is inherently an integral part of a man, and it was the Creator's intention to have them as mutual, dependent coequals. Following creation, God called Adam and Eve coequals and affirmed that they are bound to live together and complement each other's needs, although as a sovereign and orderly Creator, he assigned them different roles. Mutual dependence and respect between man and woman constitute a sacred covenant ordained by God Almighty since creation. Alas, self-proclaimed feminists such as you, call yourselves "champions of women's rights", redefine the established orderly and equitable covenant that God made man and woman enter into in the beginning. Oftentimes, people oppose Christianity on the ground that it is a biased belief that lowers women to an inferior status, without acknowledging that the Creator champions the equality of both genders.

Dear friend, let me assure you that the God I serve places equal value on men and women and established societal and familial order from the beginning. Consider the life of Jesus Christ, for instance. He was born of a virgin woman whom the angel told "Hail, thou that art highly favoured, the Lord is with thee: blessed are thou among women."[7]Jesus Christ treated women with remarkable dignity and utmost respect on numerous occasions,

5. See Isaiah 53.

6. Genesis 2:21–24 (KJV).

7. Luke 1:28 (KJV).

including the sinning woman who came crying while washing his feet with her tears and hair[8], and his resurrection which was witnessed first by a woman—not his male disciples.[9] Don't pay attention to the vain words of men. Look at people from the standpoint of love and equality according to God instead of advancing groundless counterarguments based on flawed views of the naturalists and feminists. Only the Bible offers a greater sense of equality and acceptance to humans, regardless of race, gender, and ethnicity; for it is given to them by God Almighty.

I trust that you are making progress in your quest for truth.

May the Lord continue to show you grace and mercy and draw you close to himself.

Best regard,
The Lord's servant

8. See Luke 7: 37–50.
9. See Matthew 28.

6

Atrocities in the Bible and Longevity

Sunday, May 15, 1994
1939 Bemba Road
Kamda, Earthly Domain

Brother Melchizedek,

I have delayed my response because I feel as if I am communicating with a brick wall. I have never met a Christian that is so stubborn and has such a zeal as yours to defend his mythical thoughts—it is indeed frustrating! You have indeed gone above and beyond the limits of logic to defend the indefensible. You tried your very best to defend who you call Jesus, the Christ, although I still think he is a fictional character. What I find very intriguing is what you share about the Book of Psalms. I do not believe in the inerrancy of the Bible, but there is a high level of thinking in this passage, for it talks about a meeting supposedly held in eternity past. One can only imagine that such an author would fare much better if he devoted his time to worthy literature instead of a mythical book.

I have done a brief research on your Bible in the interim and concluded that you worship a violent and genocidal God who committed mass murder. I was appalled by what is recorded in the Old Testament and realized that your God does not make a distinction between those who belong to him and their enemies. Indeed, mass murder is not only committed against those who lived in the land of Canaan but also the Israelites who were supposed to be on your God's side. I gave up on reading the Bible when I got to the Book of Nahum and have no desire to go back and read about the horrors I encountered while reading. Notwithstanding I am well-equipped to debunk your pathetic claims about your God; you have certainly made a big mistake in assuming that I am a gullible person who accepts any claim without verifying the arguments presented, based on the scientific method. I am a highly educated individual with an array of resources at my disposal. I am more than capable to confidently stand my ground.

The irony of your letters thus far is that you claim to espouse the notion of a singular God, irrespective of science, but have the audacity to tell me that I am full of pride. How pathetic! I am the humblest person in the world as far as I am concerned, and I concede defeat only when empirical, convincing evidence is presented. So far the case you attempt to make for creation (garden of Eden) has failed, for our Neanderthal forefathers lived in Africa millions of years ago, and the absurd biblical account of creation does not permit procreation (Adam probably did not have daughters). Moreover, it is unrealistic to assume that the seven billion humans who inhabit Earth come from two forefathers (Adam and Eve).

One of the greatest impediments to the human quest for civilization and modernization is religion, and the institution of slavery drew a great deal of inspiration from the Christian religion, as some Christians in position of leadership consented to such tragedies. Similarly, various societies were discouraged from striving to make meaningful contribution to modernization by religion; they were rather encouraged to spend a great deal of time entertaining the fictional idea of God, and whenever a challenge arises, they pray instead of seeking tangible solutions. Consequently, it was the societies without religion that made incredible leaps in medicine, education, and politics.

I have more questions to ask but I will allow you to respond to the objections I raised in this letter before you can scramble for responses to my next inquiries.

Wake up fool!
Marawi, the Atheist

Thursday, June 2, 1994
1517 Year Zero BCE Road
Paradise, God's Kingdom

Brother Marawi Njerabé,

G reetings in the name of the Lord and blessings in the name of Jesus
Christ. Thank you for your continued willingness to communicate
with me .

You have made progress in your quest for truth since you embarked
on this journey a little over a year ago, despite the frustration you expressed
in your last letter. I understand your aggravation because the truth of the
Word of God is confronting the lies that the enemy has stored in your mind.
I am going to provide some clarifications in this note and am confident
that you will meditate on the counterperspectives I offer regarding the deep
questions of life. The Lord is resolved to help you come to understand him
and ultimately have a personal relationship with him.

You cherry-picked certain verses in the Old Testament to reinforce
your established notion of a violent and immoral God. In doing this, you
fail to understand the Bible as a piece of historical literature. When one
reads a piece of literature, one cannot make a conclusion until the text is
read in its entirety and the facts are examined. Similarly, God's beautiful
story of creation and plan of salvation can only be properly understood
when the entire Bible is read and analyzed. Second, because you are pre-
disposed to despise the Christians and their God, you failed to read the
Bible in context. A wise man once said: "A text without a context becomes
a pretext."[1] If you read the Bible simply to debunk the points I made and
the existence of God instead of reading it as an objective reader, then the
Spirit of God cannot reveal his mysteries to you. Furthermore, the so-called
terrifying stories in the Old Testament reflect the heart of man (sin) and
are meant to show humans that God is holy and does not tolerate sin. The
wickedness of the Canaanites and sometimes the Israelites tend to be ignored (child sacrifice, sexual immorality, murder, idolatry, among others),
and God's justice and righteousness are demonstrated in his judgment, for
he gave justice to both the Jew and Gentile accordingly. This argument is,
without a doubt, a one-sided argument because the other side of the argument is never examined and considered: What about the millions of Jews

---

1. Ravi Zacharias

and Christians who suffered and continue to suffer at the hands of the Assyrians, Babylonians, Romans, Japanese, Muslims, and secular and atheist leaders such as Joseph Stalin, Vladimir Lenin, Pol Pot, and Mao Zedong? Recent global surveys on religious persecution revealed that eight in ten persecutions worldwide are directed at Christians, yet there is no outcry in the media or academia about this. The irony is that the same people who claim to not believe in God unless he manifests himself in a physical form are the same ones who criticize him when he upholds justice. Third, you made an assertion that condemns God but failed to use the same standard to examine your atheistic position. Indeed, if the same arguments that are used to judge Christianity are applied to evaluate atheism, you would realize that atheism is far worse simply because of the shear havoc it has caused. Moreover, there is no moral reference point in evolution and by extension atheism: it only deals with survival and self-preservation. Therefore, the standard of judgment that you use to criticize God is a theistic notion, for moral law necessitates a supreme law giver who dictates the standards. In fact, if God does not exist, there is no reference point for morality; the interpretation of morality and immorality become relative—not absolute.

In Christianity, there is a widely understood teaching known as dispensation—a window or period of time during which man is tested in respect of obedience to some specific revelation concerning the will of God. There are seven dispensations: Innocence (Adam and Eve in the garden of Eden before the fall); Conscience (after Adam and Eve sin, and are thus no longer innocent but accountable for their actions); Human Government (humans came together after the flood and formed nations, such as the one led by Nimrod—it continues to this day); Promise (God made a promise to Abraham that his posterity will be great and possess the land of Canaan in the Levant); Law (the children of Israel left Egypt under the guidance of Moses and received laws from God, including the Ten Commands); Grace (Jesus Christ came and died on the cross; the veil is torn for gentiles to come in and get saved); Millennial Kingdom of Christ (Christ will return and rule from Jerusalem, believers will be a part of his kingdom). It is important to understand that each dispensation ends in judgment as man has failed every time in keeping God's command in light of what he revealed. With this in mind, the atrocities you speak of all follow the Dispensation of Innocence and preceded the Dispensation of Grace. They came about as a result of direct rebellion of what God revealed to man and shall cease at the Lord's appointed time.[2]

You are inconsistent in the way you reject God, the author of your life. In a previous letter, you rejected the notion of religion and God as a whole, but now it is evident that you entertain other myths about creation but not the Christian account in the garden of Eden. Well, Marawi, what's wrong and bizarre with creation in the garden of Eden? You stated that it is unrealistic to say that the seven billion or so humans who populate Planet Earth come from Adam and Eve, and that the idea that Adam has sons and daughters who intermarried is absurd. If this is the premise on which you judge the Christian view of creation, you have also tacitly rejected evolution. The big bang theory and other scientific theories all point to a starting point; therefore, there must be a single original organism from which procreation commenced. Moreover, pseudoscience is quick to claim that the universe and the earth are billions of years old. Human history, however, is generally accepted to be between 5,000 and 7,000 years, though this vast chasm happens to not bother them. The logical conclusion based on pseudoscience is that the Earth should be overpopulated by now since humans have been living on it for millions of years. The world population, however, did not reach one billion until the nineteenth century, and in a mere 200 years, it has already exceeded seven billion people. No one can, therefore, logically conclude that humans have inhabited the Earth for millions of years. The family of Jacob went to Egypt as seventy persons but left with more than two million souls at the time of Exodus 400 years later. Let that sink in!

I fervently wish you understand God's mercy and what it means to be created in the image of God. Indeed, you are deeply entrenched in atheism and have been brainwashed to believe that there is nothing beyond your present, physical life to the extent that you cannot wrap your mind around God's plan of salvation for mankind and what it means to be human. Your demand that the Lord physically show himself begs the response of Jesus Christ when the Pharisees insisted on a sign from heaven: "A wicked and adulterous generation seeketh after a sign; and there shall be no sign be given unto it, but the sign of the prophet Jonas."[3] Moreover, your constant rejection of the existence of God places you at a greater condemnation than those who are part of Satan's kingdom, for the Bible says: "Thou

2. See I Corinthians 9:17; Ephesians 1:10; Ephesians 3: 2; Colossians 1:25.

3. Matthew 16:4 (KJV).

believest that there is one God; thou doest well: the devils also believe, and tremble."[4] The distinction between Satan and God is comparable to darkness and light, or the east and west, but Satan and his cohort of devils acknowledge the existence of God, for they tremble at his presence. You, on the other hand, have refused to profess his name and acknowledge him, despite overwhelming evidence and the fact that I am still alive and communicating with you after my earthly sojourn—thanks to the Lord. You are, therefore, at fault and without excuse, for Jesus Christ said that ". . . For unto whomsoever much is given, of him shall be much required . . ."[5]

The beauty of God is that he loves all humans, including renegades. You continuously speak ill of him and sin every day, yet he destroys you not. However, God's patience is not a sign of weakness and inaction, for if you remain stiff-necked till death or the rapture, it will be eternally too late to repent. The Lord will cast you into the lake of fire with the devil who is the author of your belief—atheism.

Cordially yours,
The Lord's servant, Melchizedek

Saturday, July 9, 1994
1939 Bemba Road
Kamda, Earthly Domain

Melchizedek,

I appreciate that despite my frank and sometimes harsh tone against your flawed arguments, you're still in contact with me. I, however, take offense at the false claim that I am neither the author of my life nor the guarantor thereof. Let me assure you, I am indeed the author of my life and the guarantor of its continuation. You, dear friend, an avid follower and believer in your God, passed away twelve years ago at the tender age of thirty-seven. I am presently fifty years old and was told by my doctor last week when I went in for my regular medical check-up that I definitely have at least forty more years to live. If God is the author of life, why did he not give you longevity? As you can see, I control my own destiny instead

4. James 2:19 (KJV).
5. Luke 12:48 (KJV).

52

of relying on a certain God. In keeping an optimal health, I go to the gym regularly, eat healthy, and get adequate rest. These habits alone suffice to guarantee my next breath. I am also an avid fan of positive thinking and have no doubt that whatever I set my mind on to achieve will come to fruition. In this regard, prior studies, data, and my conviction point to a life of up to one hundred years.

You made strange claims in your letter, abasing me below Satan and his devils. Know that your attempt to intimidate me has failed and I am the more emboldened to remain an atheist. I deem it inexpedient to reply to the nonsensical words you uttered, accusing me of cherry-picking, and the illogical objections you attempted to find in my worldview. Stop mentioning your God's mercy and love, for they are null and void in my dictionary. I do not believe in them nor need them. Christianity and the Bible should be banned in academia and beyond.

Enough said today!

Your frustrated friend,
Marawi

Saturday, August 13, 1994
1517 Year Zero BCE Road
Paradise, God's Kingdom

My friend,

I trust that you are in excellent health. You believe that because I died at a much younger age than you ought to be regarded negatively and proves that the life of man and his next breath are in his own hands. Paul said, "We are confident, I say, and willing rather to be absent from the body, and to be present with the Lord."[6] And King Solomon said: "Boast not thyself of tomorrow; for thou knowest not what a day may bring forth."[7] These mean that although God made us the keeper of our earthly body, he does not hand us the key to immortality. God is not against you going to the gym and visiting doctors for check-ups, but claiming that you and your team of doctors can determine how long your life would last is nothing short of

---

6. 2 Corinthians 5:8 (KJV).
7. Proverbs 27:1 (KJV).

foolishness and absurdity. If sickness is taken out of the equation, there are still a myriad of ways that death can overcome you: accident, murder, slip and fall, tornadoes, or simply giving up the ghost while sleeping. Contrary to your belief, I delight that the Lord called me home so that I no longer endure the suffering of mortals, for I serve an eternal Creator in whose eyes one thousand years is as one day. You are pondering the possibility of one hundred years of life—I live in eternity.

Moreover, your argument bears little credibility because since the dawn of civilization, mankind has been unsuccessfully seeking the key to immortality. In the quest of eternal life, some sought the magical effect of elixir, while others put their faith in other mortals such as doctors and witches, to no avail. Jesus declared: "I am the resurrection, and the life: he that believeth in me, though he were dead, yet shall he live: And whosoever liveth and believeth in me shall never die. Believest thou this?"[8] I thank God for gathering me to himself at a young age so that I no longer had to witness the wickedness of man, and I can enjoy the blessings heaven offers. Dear friend, you have no idea what it is like to behold the glory and majesty of Jesus Christ the Son and God the Father. I marvel at their glorious greatness daily and the blessings of paradise that far exceed human comprehension. You, on the other hand, are blinded by Satan and misguided by the lie that earthly life is all that there is since death is a place of oblivion and nothingness. I can assure you that life is merely a transitional period for those who die believing in the Lamb of God. Words cannot express the glory of heaven and the wonders God reserved for those who choose to commune with him. Brother Marawi, since you don't have the supreme and eternal authority over you, you are terrified by the inevitability of death and embrace vain hope; ". . . for dust thou art, and unto dust shalt thou return . . ."[9] I, on the other hand, have a well-established and grounded hope: a hope beyond the grave that I can boldly and reliably attest to.

The Lord knows that you endorse the total boycott and banning of Christian doctrine in academia and beyond. How ironic is that, comrade? You who repeatedly profess to be a free thinker, tolerant of diverse ideas, have singled out Christianity and called for its suppression and abolition. I highly recommend that you humble yourself and seek not an affront with God Almighty, for those who try to eliminate Christianity eventually pass away, but the gospel message of Christ prevails. Who would have predicted

8 John 11:25–26 (KJV).

9. Genesis 3:19

that the fastest growing underground churches in the world would be in China and Iran—two nations vehemently opposed to the preaching and proliferation of the gospel. One leader in China went as far as proclaiming the utter annihilation of Christianity in China, as he declared it "a thing of the past,"[10] while not realizing that a few decades later, this nation would be on the path to become the most populous nation of believers of Christ in the world. Behold, his body lies dead in the grave but the gospel message prevails! Christianity always prospers in an atmosphere of enforced and institutionalized persecutions so do not fool yourself into believing otherwise. Your disdain of Christianity is the work of the devil that has hardened your heart to a point of utter hatred for your fellow human beings.

Brotherly affection,
Melchizedek

10. Mao Zedong

7

Abortion

Sunday, September 4, 1994
1939 Bemba Road
Kamda, Earthly Domain

My friend,

I picked up your letter last Wednesday but could not read it right away or reply to your objections in a timely fashion because I was on a business trip to Czechoslovakia. It was indeed a very fun trip, but I choose not to share the details of the trip with you, lest your narrow-minded brain leads you to judge me. I appreciate the fact that you seem to care for me, but I would never share with you the things I am in need of because you serve an imaginary God, and I do not believe neither you nor the entity you venerate can change the outcome of my circumstances. I am not going to apologize for the comment I made concerning your passing. Since your passing, I have never seen you face to face so I cannot affirm that your passing was expedient. One thing is certain: I am still alive and in great physical and mental health. I enjoy my wealth, family, and friends, while your bones are rotting in the coffin at the Nangyo Cemetery in Ngonnba Quarter, N'Djamena. The fictitious description of the place you dwell in and the supposed failure of man to obtain the key to immortality also certainly do not help your case. As far as I am concerned, the dead know nothing and cannot enjoy life. Similarly, no apology will be offered concerning the comments I made in regard to Christianity in academia. I unapologetically call for the limitation of dangerous doctrines such as Christianity in all educational institutions.

I believe that this is enough mention of the rubbish in your previous letter. I would, however, like to leave you with a question so that you can address it in your next letter. Is your God a pro-abortionist or anti-abortionist.

I have a good idea about what position you will take on this, and naturally that of your God, but I want my suspicions to be confirmed by you.

Bye!
Njerabé Marawi

Friday, October 7, 1994
1517 Year Zero BCE Road
Paradise, God's Kingdom

My dear brother,

I am happy you are in excellent health. You made disrespectful comments concerning my passing, but I forgive you, as Christ would have done. As for matters related to life and death, dear brother, do not venture into assumptions for you will discover the truth when your life on Earth comes to an end. Charles Darwin, Stephen Hawking, Pol Pot, Mao Zedong, Christopher Hitchens, Joseph Stalin and many other atheists had spoken as you presently do but now face the reality of the God they despise, with no way out or back—academia and legislation cannot put an end to the teachings of Christ, for God is in control and truth cannot remain hidden.

Now, I would like to tackle your inquiry regarding human choice in one of the controversies in politics. First, you would like to know if God is pro-abortionist or anti-abortionist. To place the Lord on a particular side in politics is certainly not a good idea, because politics is an institution started by man, thus naturally flawed. What I can say with unerring certainty, however, is that God's position on abortion is uncomplicated and clear. Yet it is seemingly a conundrum for secularists who repeatedly sow discord to discredit Christianity, since it openly disapproves of abortion, which is synonymous with infanticide. The first mistake is that people misdefine the terms *freedom* and *freewill*. The Lord granted both privileges to humans (freedom and freewill), but absolute freedom is exclusively reserved for the

Creator, and any attempt to institute it in your fallen domain will end up in chaos; anarchy is the end thereof. When pro-choice activists and their respective constituents affirm that a woman has the discretion to keep or dispose of her infant since it is her body, they undoubtedly fail to understand that another person's life is involved—not just that of the mother. God told the prophets Isaiah and Jeremiah that he knew them before they were conceived in their mothers' wombs.[1] God also spoke to Rebecca thus: "Two nations are in thy womb"[2]—not two products of conception—thus irrefutably demonstrating that life starts prior to birth. Furthermore, the Almighty spoke of the coming of several mighty prophets in the Bible prior to their birth, including Samson, Samuel, John the Baptist, and Jesus Christ. This established fact that can be found throughout the Bible offers a clear rebuke to those who claim to be Christian but support abortion and the pro-abortionists who claim that the fetus cannot be considered human until fully developed and delivered. It is indeed ironic that those who profess an ardent passion to fight for human rights are the same ones who push to rob others of the dignity and sanctity of life. How tragic! Make no mistake, dear friend, abortion equates to murder not only in my sight, but in the sight of the Lord as well. How can the giver of life hate life? Suppose your mother elected to abort you, you would never have a chance to be alive and enjoy the pleasures that you are claiming to indulge in. There is a reason why God said life is sacred and ought not to be taken lightly.[3] The Almighty elevated the life of humans above all his creation and created them in his image. Animals, though typically portrayed as beings without the ability to think and reason do not abort their young. Humans, on the other hand, claim to possess the highest degree of intellect, yet cannot fully comprehend what it means to be human nor grasp the concept of the sacredness of life. How pathetic and tragic!

One of the most successful instruments of deception, utilized by the enemy is to blind people who lack faith in God with a false sense of boldness and empowerment, as they challenge the orderly status quo established by the Father. Having said that, women who choose abortion, for example, claim to be independent and have total emancipation from their male counterparts because in their estimation, they are unhindered by societal norms and expectations. Indeed, such women and their accomplices—parents, a

1. See Jeremiah 1:5; Isaiah 49:5.
2. See Genesis 25:23
3. See Exodus 21: 22–25

significant other, and physicians—are convinced that the option to keep or get rid of an infant is solely a personal matter. The reality, however, is different: a baby's life is not only a personal matter but a life that involves a number of indispensable actors, of whom God is the most important and the supreme authority. When a woman gets pregnant, whether voluntarily or involuntarily, her body is used as a vehicle through which a life is going to enter Planet Earth. Pregnancy does not only signal change for a woman, but also that of the future father, immediate family, and friends. Ideally, the man responsible for the pregnancy prepares himself mentally and financially to raise the child. The woman's parents and friend shave an equally important role to play in the future of the child: they can offer critical advice on how to raise a child to the soon-to-be mother, contribute as babysitters to alleviate the stress of raising a baby, and share the essentials of motherhood with her. As for God, he allows the coming of one of his recent creatures to the land of men. In sending that person, whether male or female, they have a purpose to fulfill: some are called to be doctors, others preachers, and leaders, and still others social workers. The prospect of abortion and single parenthood constitute one of the reasons why the Bible is against practices such as divorce, fornication, and women and men living together without formally getting married, often referred to as partnership. This discussion goes back to our previous exchange regarding man's rebellion against God's commandments. Being aware of man's heart and the consequences that result from defiant decisions that are not in line with his Word, the Father established clear guidelines to prevent abortion and other familial issues that are sadly ignored by humans. Be assured that abortion is just one of the sins that can be averted if the instructions of God are heeded, for there would be no fornication, no adultery, and no divorce.

Proponents of abortion also claim that certain parents are under unimaginable and unbearable financial constraint. Therefore, it is simply infeasible to raise a child; thus, abortion is a more desirable alternative. The cost of parenting can be overwhelming, but people who reason thus are not true believers in the Christian God, for He has unlimited resources to provide for parents and child (Jehovah-Jireh). The Bible gives examples of infants and individuals that parents and society deem unworthy that were transformed by God, who performed awesome wonders through them. Read about the lives of Jephthah and Moses as examples.[4] The Bible says: "Humble yourselves

---

4. See Exodus 1–2; Judges 11.

therefore under the mighty hand of God, that he may exalt you in due time: Casting all your care upon him; for he careth for you."[5]

God's love is unconditional and merciful. He is unchanging. Although the terms are *premature* or *unplanned* pregnancy, the fact of the matter is that such incidents are symptomatic of the bigger and deeper problem, which is sin. If repentance is made with a sincere heart, God is always faithful and just to forgive the sins of humans and offer ways to help them overcome the consequences of their sins and those of others that affect them. It's ironic that when trying times such as an unwanted pregnancy strike as a result of fornication or rape, instead of turning to God for guidance in prayer, most women and their accomplices try to seek their own solution and take matters into their own hands. There is no safer ground than the eye of the storm—God is still sovereign in the midst of a storm. Indeed, I serve the God who can move in mysterious ways to preserve the life of a young, innocent, to-be-born baby, including provision to the concerned parents, adoption, and assistance via social programs.

Last, aside from the utter and obvious offense to the Father, abortion has consequences. Despite the effectiveness of modern technology to murder infants at a much faster pace, bareness, the contraction of diverse sicknesses, difficulty to give birth in the future, and the fact that a great number of women have died while attempting to abort an unborn baby are some examples of direct consequences of this malicious practice. Doctors, nonmedical personnel, and whosoever consciously consents verbally or tacitly to the execution of abortion is equally guilty as the woman committing the abortion. There is no lesser sin in the eyes of the Lord, and as children of God, each person is accountable to the Lord for not rebuking a brother or sister when their decision is not in line with the Word of God. To see evil and not speak out against it is the same as being the perpetrator thereof—not to speak *is* to speak.

Best regards,
Your loyal friend and brother, Melchizedek

5. I Peter 5: 6–7 (KJV).

8

Homosexuality, Transgenderism, and the LGBTQ Movement

Saturday, November 26, 1994
1939 Bemba Road
Kamda, Earthly Domain

Dear conceited friend,

I read your pitiful letter warning me of the consequence of what shall follow me if I continue to speak the truth of your passing. None of your warnings move me. You died a very young man and that is lamentable. I do not want to convert to your belief if it does not promise longevity, for I love this life and would like to live forever if possible. The psychological warfare that you have been waging is reaping an adverse result. I will continue to advocate for the abolition of Christianity in academia.

I read your reply about the question I posed concerning abortion and much of your answer did not surprise me, for in your distorted worldview, you deem that the lives of mortals are transcendent because they are created in the image of a certain God. I am disappointed, however, that your response is partial as you and your God have no regard for woman's right to do what she wants with her body—something we, the highly evolved intellectual support. It is only logical to fully support women's right to have control over their bodies since there is no God, and no intrinsic value to human life. What a backward Dark Age coward!

It is only fitting to ask you the next question that has been on my mind—and that of many others for a long time—namely, Is your God for homosexuality or against it? Would gays and transgenders (the LGBTQ community) make it to heaven? Unlike you, I am a free-thinking man who accepts everyone, regardless of their racial and sexual orientation.

I look forward to hear what you and your God have to say about this fundamental civil right.

In the name of human rights,
Marawi Njerabé

~

Wednesday, December 7, 1994
1517 Year Zero BCE Road
Paradise, God's Kingdom

Mon frère bien-aimé,

You asked about the Lord's position on abortion, and I answered your question. Instead of examining my response, you heap insults on me. This tactic is treacherous and is certainly designed to intimidate and discourage those who hold divergent opinions from you. Now that I am preparing to answer your subsequent question, I trust that your attitude will change, and you will examine my answer more carefully.

You enquired about God's position on same-sex marriage. The Lord instructed me to make one thing clear: The question ought to be about *who* a person is rather than what he or she is and does (humans are created in the image of God). First and foremost, God loves all his children equally and being gay does not disqualify one from the love of the Creator. Ultimately, it is unrepentance and unbelief that brings about condemnation. Homosexuality, gender reassignment, and bisexualism are just symptoms of a bigger and deeper problem. This problem is a three-letter word that no one wants to hear about: sin. God is holy and therefore cannot tolerate sin. If the Christian God was indifferent in regard to same-sex marriage and the transgender movement, then he would have made it clear from the beginning. When God saw that Adam was lonely, he could've made another Adam (the same gender) to be his helper and companion, but instead the Lord elected to create the opposite gender. He then joined the two in a sacred covenant and stated that they were divinely ordained to live together forever, as husband and wife. Later when God chose the children of Israel as the instrument through which he would bring the good news to the entire world (gentiles), he made his position on same-sex marriage very clear in the Old Testament and the New Testament.[1]

Proponents of same-sex marriage usually argue that God is a loving God, and therefore he cannot condemn this evil practice. They also argue that there is no explicit verse in the Bible that speaks against homosexuality despite ample objection in the Scriptures. I would submit to you, however, that since God is love, he must hate. God loves children; therefore, he hates abortion. God loves holiness; therefore, he hates sin. God loves the sanctity of marriage; therefore, he hates divorce. Now, dear friend, as for you, I trust you will examine the passages I shared above and make an honest conclusion, independent of emotional tendencies. God said, "Thou shalt not lie with mankind, as with womankind: it is abomination."[2] God also said, "If a man also lie with mankind, as he lieth with a woman, both of them have committed an abomination . . ."[3]Later on, the Lord cautioned the children of Israel against the consequence of sin, including homosexuality as he says: "Defile not ye yourselves in any of these things: for in all these the nations are defiled which I cast out before you: And the land is defiled: therefore I do visit the iniquity thereof upon it, and the land itself vomiteth out her inhabitants."[4] Make no mistake, unless humanity heeds the commands of God that govern courtship and marriage, judgment is on the way. Just like other sins, the effeminate seek reasons to justify themselves instead of being broken, and kneeling and asking God for forgiveness and deliverance. The cliché excuse of homosexuals is, "I cannot help who I am." or "I am born this way"—thereby forgetting that God is not the author of confusion, and no saved person is to give in to the desires, thoughts, and temptations of the flesh.

Further, what is often misunderstood in discussions surrounding this controversy is the fact that like a father who loves his child, although God's love for humans is unfathomable, he also corrects the misdeeds of his children. Every good father wishes the best for his son or daughter. When they

---

1. See Leviticus 18:22; Deuteronomy 22:5; Romans 1:26–27; I Corinthians 6: 9; I Timothy 1: 9–10.

2. Leviticus 18: 22;

3. Leviticus 20:13

4. Leviticus 18:24–25 (KJV).

steal, lie, or make wrong decisions, a parent does not wink at their wrongs and look the other way. Quite the contrary, a good parent will do whatever it takes to bring his child back to the right path. Likewise, if God truly loves his children, he cannot tolerate homosexuality which goes against the orderly relationship he instituted between a man and a woman from the beginning. It is the so-called free thinkers such as you who imagine the Creator as an unsecured entity that needs the approval of his creatures. Indeed, one the most fundamental blunders that the living make is that they think whatever fits in their agenda and limited mind must be what God stand for as well. The Lord is immutable, omnipresent, omniscient, and omnipotent. Let that sink in your mind!

The Bible says that human wisdom is foolishness to the Lord,[5] for his knowledge and wisdom surpass that of mortal man in an incomparable manner. Some secular, pro-same-sex activists claim that they cannot accept a God who is a bigot and full of hatred for those who chose to pursue a romantic relationship with individuals of the same gender. They thus deem themselves tolerant and accepting. One thing is certain: God loves man and that's why he rebukes him of his sin, as any loving and loyal friend would. These same activists do not truly love homosexuals, however, because they are more concerned with telling them what they want to hear and what makes them feel good rather than giving them the truth; thus misleading them as they face God when they depart the land of the living. The Bible says, "And ye shall know the truth, and the truth shall make you free."[6]It's no exception in this case. God Almighty does not need anyone to testify to his majesty, neither does he need mortal man's approval. When he made solemn promises in the Bible, God always swore by his own name: I Am,[7] implying that there is no name greater than his. His name indicates that he was, is, and shall be. It's God who created the universe and man, not the other way around. God's stance on marriage and same-sex marriage does not change, despite the prevailing heresies of those who are beguiled by the devil to believe in the hedonistic lie of "Do as you wish, God loves you anyway." He is the same God who declared, "Heaven and earth shall pass away, but my words shall not pass away."[8]

5. See I Corinthians 1: 25; I Corinthians 3: 19.
6. John 8:32 (KJV).
7 See Exodus 3:14
8. Matthew 24: 35 (KJV).

In addition, homosexuality also poses an existential threat to humanity, though proponents of same-sex marriage affirm that this devil-inspired practice does not cause any harm to humanity and can exist in society peaceably. The sustained blatant lie that sodomy is unharmful is another instrument used by the enemy to turn God's children away from the noble path he has established for them. For the sake of this discussion, let's imagine a world where homosexuality is universally accepted, and every single couple is made up of individuals of the same gender. Be assured that in such a scenario, that society would cease to exist within decades. Indeed, certain countries with low birthrate have felt the burden of homosexuality on their social fabric and economy. Others have gone as far as banning same-sex marriage in order to preserve the survival and relevance of their nation on the global stage. Dear Marawi, homosexuality is not only a problem of Christians and their God, but also that of the so-called secular world, for even in your worldview, survival and reproduction are paramount.

I hope and trust that you will take the biblical stance on relationship and marriage seriously.

Sincerely yours,
Melchizedek.

Saturday, December 17, 1994
1939 Bemba Road
Kamda, Earthly Domain

Hello!

I read your letter and am writing to express my counterperspective to your stance on homosexuality. First, I categorically reject all your attempts to explain the inherent nature of man as sinful and the various arguments that you offered to justify the existence of your mythical God. You tried to offer an explanation as to why your God opposes same-sex marriage. In doing so, you affirmed that in order to address the issue of same-sex marriage, one has to ask the question of who the person is rather than what the person is. To this end, you defended your view in that humans are created in the image of God, which therefore sets the precedence and guidance on how to define one's gender and options in dating. This explanation, however, bears little credibility because you have thus far failed to offer a convincing argument regarding the existence of your God and how he created humans. If God loves gays as you claim, then why would it be wrong for them to choose a partner of the same gender? You further stated that homosexuality, gender reassignment, and bisexualism are only symptomatic of a deeper problem, and that predicament is regarded as your preconceived notion of sin. Let me assure you that these desired ideals are symptomatic of nothing. They reflect the longings of a collective group to have an honorable and dignified position in society in order to live a full, free life. I also reject your recourse to the Bible, particularly the fairytale of Adam and Eve and the supposed commandments given to the Israelites, to reinforce your regrettable position on these sensitive issues. I will never accept the Bible as a credible source of argument. It's not worth my time and any argument that comes from it becomes automatically null and void in my estimation.

I am also appalled by the remark you made, stating that your God's unparalleled love does not translate into letting humans do as they wish and see fit. You noted that as a holy and a just God, he is obligated to reprimand his creation and set them on the path of righteousness. Why is that? I have news for you: If your God truly exists, he must accord the freedom of choice regarding dating, marriage, and gender to his creation. It just does not make sense to imagine a God that acts like a man with a big stick (dictator) and gets involved in the business of his creatures that he supposedly loves. Deities are busy and suppose to leave their creatures alone. Your analogy of a father-to-son relationship to explain your reprehension and suppression of liberal position, vis-à-vis the LGBTQ movement, also fails miserably. Your comparison of an imaginary God to real human life is lamentable. Fathers and sons interact in a direct and tangible manner, whereas your God cannot and will not interact with his creation directly.

When advocating for the rights of homosexuals, we intellectuals do no invoke the wisdom of a deity but rather fully rely on our own judgment. It is foolish that you affirmed that the wisdom of your God far surpasses that of humans. In reality, it is the activists you criticized that love homosexuals, for we accept their lifestyle and do not pass on judgment on them.

Last, you exaggerated the matter at hand, claiming that homosexuality represents an existential threat to humanity. Melchizedek, where is evidence for your claim? I don't know what planet you reside in but in this planet called earth, this will never happen. Conversely, what represents an existential threat is the targeting and persecution of homosexuals and pro-homosexual activists.

I do not expect you to have much to say about this topic.

Talk to you later,
Marawi

Tuesday, December 27, 1994
1517 Year Zero BCE Road
Paradise, God's Kingdom

Brother Marawi,

G od must reprimand humans and set them on the path of righteous-ness because he cares for their soul, and wants to spare their soul from destruction. God is neither ordinary deity nor a dictator. His nature requires justice, and his unfathomable love makes him interact with humans. Throughout the Scripture and the history of man, one can see that when man is allowed to sin (including homosexuality), he often becomes emboldened, gets bored of that sin, and looks for ways to render his actions worse and more wicked in order to increase the false sense of pleasure he derives therein. Having said that, the LGBTQ movement started with individuals demanding freedom to court and make intragender marriage socially acceptable. Society's disregard of the biblical stance on the issue and decreasing persecution of same-sex couples were also motivating factors. Howbeit, as one can predict from any movement that is not grounded in the Word of God, it has grown to a satanic society in which gender can change day by day, hour by hour, minute by minute. Doctors are also allowed to perform surgery on men and women in order to alter the biological makeup they are endowed with by the Lord. It is also becoming commonly accepted that children, whose cognitive faculties are not fully developed, can decide what gender they wish to be and surgeries are performed accordingly, because parents are discouraged from teaching them the proper way instituted by the Creator. Dear friend, homosexuality is evil at its finest, and a holy God cannot and will not tolerate such an act.

In Genesis 3, the serpent said unto the woman (Eve) that she "shall not surely die" if she ate of the forbidden fruit. He further stated: "For God doth know that in the day ye eat thereof, then your eyes shall be opened, and ye shall be as gods, knowing good and evil." Satan himself was an angel of God who lost his position in heaven because of his desire to take the place of God. He was banished, and likewise, when the woman decided to do what was right in her eyes, in spite of God's warning, she brought about all manner of evil and suffering on earth. The moral of this biblical account is this: any society that decides to play God and do what is right according its own wicked desires will lose its sense of shame and come to utter destruction and judgment.

You are deceived in believing that the subject at hand does not pose an existential threat to humanity. You argue that encouraging children (who literally represent the next generation) to be homosexual or whatever they desire to be is fine, and that abortion is totally acceptable. Well, dear friend, have you examined the cost? A generation that accepts ideas without analyzing their long-term consequences, coupled with the increase of people identifying as transgender, bisexuals, and gays, equals a degenerate society that is in decline. You also seem to be at ease with gender reassignment (including to children) and affirm that the proliferation of these movements reflects the collective desire of society. You thus prove God's point that the heart of man is bound to sin. This is the very reason, despite freewill and freedom, humanity desperately needs the Word of God to keep humans from destroying themselves, both physically and metaphysically. Majority and popularity do not equate to morality. The guideline to doing right is the revealed will of God (the Bible), and a society that allows confusion—especially in its innocent youth—needs just that.

Contrary to popular belief, ordinary citizens who speak out against homosexuality and transgenderism—or refuse to have their integrity tainted by refusing to bow down to the pressure of the so-called activists—are those who are increasingly targeted and persecuted. Governments, predominantly in nations commonly referred to as the "first world," are passing legislation to compel all citizens to accept the evil practices of same-sex marriage and transgenderism. Indeed, new genders are increasingly created and assigned to individuals. Presently, there are dozens of genders in certain countries and "wrongfully" assigning a gender to an individual can result in imprisonment. This despicable enforced evil is the pure work of the devil. It is ironic, however, that the premise on which the neo supporters of homosexuality and their like based their argument is freedom of expression—both verbal and nonverbal—yet they are striving to suppress the freedom of speech they yearn for. It's freedom of speech insofar as one chooses to support their evil agenda: any dissident view is qualified as bigotry and homophobia—God-fearing men like Israel Folau[9] are the latest victims of the fascists. Moreover, ministers and churches are being coerced into tending to the wants of homosexuals. Some churches and ministers are threatened with having their doors closed and their ministries terminated if they do not officiate same-sex marriages. Although the judicial system of your world tends to work in the favor of evilmongerers, rest assured that God sees the injustice and in his divine timing will repay each person according to their deeds.

In this age of rapidly increasing advocacy for the separation of church and state, and that of growing divides between secularism and conservatism, Christians must not misinterpret Jesus' saying, "render to Caesar the things that are Caesar's, and to God the things that are God's."[10] Some argue that this passage indicates the indispensable necessity of separation between church and state. This assessment is true in that Christianity has been used on multiple occasions to advance selfish, narcissistic agendas—and consequently many atrocities were committed in its name—but true believers must decide to take a stance when it comes to the Lord's commands: Should believers let a tyrannical government change their fundamental values or stand by their conviction and face the consequences? Will they bow to pressure or take a stand like Daniel and Jesus Christ? There is no room for lukewarmth.

Last, Satan, the mastermind behind the equality for LGBTQ and pro-choice movements, strives to distort God's intention and purpose for humanity. The controversies are presently centered on marriage, relationship, and abortion. But unless repented and God's laws regarding the sanctity of marriage are fully restored, these practices that seem to be limited in scope will be far reaching in mainstream society. They will cease to be controversial and become normal. I predict that people would demand freedom to intermarry with animals and legally take children as wives and husbands. The notion that certain people are born with certain desires that society must accommodate without reprehension, regardless of the moral implications, is just absurd. There are people who are sexually attracted to children. Should society accommodate them or show a double standard? Where

9. A former Australian rugby league player who lost his contract for sharing God's position on sin, including homosexuality.

10. Matthew 12:17 (KJV).

does one draw the line? The Bible describes such distorted realities as sin, and sin is not dealt with through accommodation. The only way sin can be dealt with effectively is through recognition, reproach, and repentance to the Lord.

The holy, just, and orderly God does not give in to human desires—he needs not the approval of man or his opinion. He dictates his precepts at will and does in fact oppose his creation when they make unwise and ungodly decisions with their bodies. Humans are created in his image and are a temple in which he is supposed to dwell. Ungodly decisions, including abortion, homosexuality, and attempting to alter the biology of an individual, represent an utter contempt for the Lord's commands. God loves his creatures unconditionally. The proper question is: who are people instead of what they are (not homosexuals but creatures fearfully made in the image of their Creator).

I look forward to receiving your response.

Love,
Melchizedek

Sunday, January 8, 1995
1939 Bemba Road
Kamda, Earthly Domain

Friend,

I received your letter and am writing to speak what is on my mind. If your God is supreme, does not need the approval and opinion of man, and can dictate his precepts at will, then why did he create mankind to worship him to start with? Indeed, he needs gullible followers such as you to advance his agenda. The advent of any myth, be it Christian, Animistic, Islamic, or Buddhist, commences with a few people that pass it from generation to generation. I guarantee you that if every single human being stops uttering the name of your God and Christianity, he will disappear and become irrelevant overnight. Further, no one becomes emboldened by postmodern demand for equality for the LGBTQ community. You seem to be out of touch with reality and are obsessed with the idea of sin. What if the LGBT community continues to push for more rights and starts to demand the right to marry their pets? I still do not see a problem with this because we live in a free society in which people are permitted to do what suits them. It's only the religious Christians that have a problem with this because they think they still live in the Middle Ages when theocracy was the norm of the day. You also seem to be ill at ease with gender reassignment and children being allowed to choose a gender other than their biological one. Well, dear Melchizedek, deal with it! It is the political reality of the day and reflects the desires of society as a whole. Of course, I do believe that gender, as understood in the traditional sense—penis equals masculinity; vagina equals femininity—is erroneous. Scientists are now arguing that the notion of one being born male or female may not be true. I would rather see young children make this decision at an earlier age because it would save them from the headache they will encounter later in life. With modern technology, doctors can do an amazing job altering genders to a point that a person can fully become the opposite gender. It is, therefore, illogical for a father to oppose the desires of his children, and let me reiterate that I am more than happy to let my children do as they wish in their romantic and sexual life. Be assured of one thing: if one of my sons or daughters realizes that he or she is homosexual (for it is biological), I would have no problem with their decision, and would be supportive of it. I love them dearly and their happiness is paramount.

You asserted that the true victims of persecution are those who oppose same-sex marriage and transgenderism. No evidence supports this allegation. Indeed, we liberals and feminists who live in advanced, democratic society are striving for the freedom of minorities, but implying that we are a cabal of intolerant bigots is inadmissible. I have never heard of those who do not subscribe to our views being persecuted for their belief—universal freedom is indeed the rule in the land. What the government persecutes is bigotry against minorities and those who refuse call transgender persons by names other than their desired, prescribed ones. Moreover, you affirm that Christians must take a stance against homosexuality and transgenderism, because it contradicts their belief. Dear brother, this is a very dangerous and a radical position that if employed, could have devastating consequences. We are already witnessing what religious bigots are doing in certain parts of the world: they refuse to provide basic services to same-sex partners, refuse to accommodate the needs of the transgender community, and show utter contempt for minority rights. These are highly sensitive members of society that need nothing short of love and the support of the community they reside in. It's therefore lamentable that you used your self-proclaimed prophets (Jesus of Nazareth and Daniel) to justify galvanizing Christians to rally against same-sex marriage. Secular authority should trump religious values, and anyone who resists the rule of law must be persecuted severely. I can already speculate that Jesus Christ's death was a direct consequence of him opposing authority, and Daniel, I suppose, ended up with the same fate.

Last, I reject the notion that Satan is the mastermind behind the LGBT movement. I do not believe in an entity called Satan. He did not, does not, and shall not exist. Like the conception of God, Satan is a human constructed character that is formulated to explain the existence of evil—just like anything good is attributed to your God. Even if Satan is real, I would rather be on his side because he allows people to enjoy much more freedom than your God. With Satan, gays and transsexuals can do as they wish, and I can live freely without being painted as a sinner. Homosexuality is a tradition that has been in practice since the dawn of time (it precedes Christianity). It's the genuine nature of men and women who wish to partner with individuals of the same gender. Therefore, you ought not to have a problem with the so-called controversy becoming a norm. In fact, my desire and my argument all along is for the integration of minorities, particularly those with sexual orientation that might be deemed deviant by a segment of society. What is the big deal with homosexuality and transsexualism? The taboos you fear might become a reality are what we who have a liberal mind desire to become a norm.

Since you claim that your God does not stoop down to human pressure, opposes his creation making unwise (ungodly) decisions with their bodies, and that our bodies are his temple—though there is zero evidence for this—I once again will not compromise my will and values to worship your God.

In the name of freedom!
Your brother, Marawi

Tuesday, February 14, 1995
1517 Year Zero BCE Road
Paradise, God's Kingdom

Greetings in the Name of the Lord!

I have thoroughly read your last letter. You seem ill at ease with the fact that God rejects the nefarious practice of same-sex marriage and gender reassignment. If you recall, I made it clear that God is sovereign and does not bow down to anyone for approval. The question that should be asked is, Who is a person? Not What is a person? If the concept of personhood is properly defined then there would be no confusion as to who people should partner with—for God is orderly, and once humans realize that they are created in his image, they will honor his will. The Lord instituted marriage from creation to be a sacred commitment between a man and a woman, although certain people would like to think otherwise. Assuming that because God is love, he should not critique the behavior of his creatures is another blunder. As a fatherly and holy God, it is his sovereign duty to show his children the right way.

In addition, your confusion of the concept of freedom persists as you demonstrated that you don't understand what it means to be free. You affirmed that it is illogical for a father to oppose the desires of his children, and that you are more than happy to let your children do as they wish in their romantic and sexual life. What needs to be defined once again is, What does it mean to be free? God offers an unparalleled and matchless freedom to his creation, but he went above and beyond to give his creation guidance against things that the devil entices them with to eventually bring about their destruction. God's guidelines are to safeguard and regulate human freedom—not to hinder it. If one of your children opted to take his life in your presence, would you allow it? Like any good parent, I am certain the answer is a resounding no! Similarly, God knows that if he does not prescribe certain guidelines to govern the misinterpretation of the freedom afforded to his creation, the end result would be destruction—not just in this life, but also in the one to come.

Indeed, you displayed hypocrisy in your assessment of the so-called advanced, democratic society that you live in. Although claiming to be entirely free, they certainly have certain limitations on the concept of freedom. As popularized by the phrase, "One's freedom ends where another's begins," are the freedoms to murder, steal, or disobey the law permitted?

These are fundamental vices that virtually all humans discourage for the well-being of their society. One can easily observe the bias against Christians in the media, and in platforms such as YouTube, Facebook, Twitter, PayPal, and GoFundMe. Christian perspectives and activists are being increasingly harassed, suppressed, and banned. The neofascists' motto is "Do anything and share anything but Jesus Christ, the Bible, and Christianity." Preachers, politicians, Christian activists and believers have all paid a heavy price. Recently, Israel Folau, a mighty warrior of the Lord lost his Twitter account, his job, and the funds his Christian brethren raised to help offset his legal fees, just because he shared a Bible verse against sin. What an illusion of justice and equality! What a hypocrisy!

Moreover, based on your statement—"If one of my sons or daughters decides to turn homosexual, I would have no problem with their decision, and would be supportive of it. I love them dearly and their happiness is paramount,"—I can assure you that you do not love your children, at least in the intended sense. There is a difference between a rebellious, grown adult who makes a conscious decision to live in accordance with his or her heart, with no regard to the commands of God, and a young child who is trying to figure out a way to define himself and answer the deep questions of life. A father's most sacred job is to teach his children right from wrong, virtue from vice. Any father, therefore, who does not do this, is unworthy of the title of father. By teaching your children the way of righteousness, you will preserve their long-term happiness that you desire, and most importantly spare their soul from eternal damnation.

You are mistaken to believe that homosexuality and transsexualism are not a big deal. In fact, I have indicated that this is a tactic of Satan to conceal his identity and complicity in every sinful decision of man. When he beguiled Eve, he made the consumption of the forbidden fruit appear as nothing but a miniscule gesture that would not have far-reaching consequences such as perpetual human separateness from the Creator and eventually death. If you study the course of the permeation of these nefarious ideas through human history, you will clearly understand how these ideas became prevalent in the mainstream culture of mankind, especially in the twenty-first century.

Dear Marawi, you uttered a blatant lie when you claimed that opponents of your ideals have never been persecuted, and that true believers standing their ground is a dangerous idea. Well, I need not look any further than your own statements for an example, that those who use any pronoun other than the preferred ones should be prosecuted, and that transgender persons are sensitive minorities that need the protection of the government. In making these statements, you made two fundamental blunders. First, persons or governments insisting on the use of a superficial term to identify homosexuals and transgenders is a breach of free speech. Second, I never advocated for violence against those who are sexually confused. In fact, the foremost message that any Christian should convey is love. Christians who use violent means to force people to repentance are not true Christians, because they lack the love of Jesus Christ and his teachings. It's stated in the Bible that if anyone claims to love God but hates his brother, he is a liar—for God is love.[11] My argument was that those who choose to take a stand for God regarding this simple—yet controversial issue to humans—must do it convincingly and remain unmoved in the face of persecution as Daniel, Isaiah, Jeremiah, Paul, and the apostles have done.

You are right that the death of Jesus resulted from him speaking out against the sinful practices of the authorities (the Judaizers and Romans) at the time. He died so that you and I can become aware of our depravity without God and receive salvation. Unfortunately, Satan blinds you because you keep stating that he does not exist and is nothing but a human construct. Let me reiterate that he is indeed real, and is the one that has been hardening your heart so that you cannot respond to the invitation of God. He makes you utter unthoughtful comments such as "Even if Satan is real, I would rather be on his side because he allows people to enjoy much more freedom than your God," "With Satan, gays and transgenders can do as they wish," and "I can live freely without being painted a sinner."

Also, you miss the purpose of God's creation of mankind. Almighty God indeed does not need the adoration of his children to exist. He created human life solely out of love for humanity and for his pleasure, as the Bible beautifully puts it: "So God created man in his own image, in the image of God created he him; male and female created he them.[12] In case you are not aware, God already had angels in heaven prior to the creation of mankind, and as his Son Jesus Christ affirmed: If humans cease to worship him, the stones will immediately do so.[13] Humans on the other hand, need

---

11 See I John 4:20

12. Genesis 1:27 (KJV).

13. See Luke 19:40

communion with God because in doing so, they find essence and meaning to their existence and live a full, dignifying life.

I share my thoughts with love. My intention is not to cause you to be angry, but rather as a loyal brother, to speak the truth.

May God Bless You!
Melchizedek

Sunday, March 12, 1995
1939 Bemba Road
Kamda, Earthly Domain

Dear Friend,

Your sustained attack on minorities disgusts me. Your hateful speech was so grave that I stopped reading your letter and put it away for some weeks. What gives you the right to bombard individuals who embrace what you deem unethical and sinful? Although I was your friend, let the truth be spoken and told: You are a dangerous man with dangerous ideas that are counterproductive to the aspired ideals of progressive men.

I shared your last letter with highly successful CEOs at a meeting last week in Copenhagen, and we all agree that you are a bigot and hatemonger. They recommend that I cut ties with you so that I do not become influenced by your dangerous ideologies. I do agree with their advice. You are indeed a bigot with dangerous ideas. I have therefore, decided to put an end to our correspondence. It is your hardheadedness and inability to see controversies from non-Christian perspective that caused me to say adieu.

This is my last letter but I hope that you change your narrow way of seeing things and sympathize more with people who are victim of religion.

Farewell.
Marawi

9

Technology

Thursday, March 23, 1995
1939 Bemba Road
Kamda, Earthly Domain

Melchizedek,

I change my mind and decided to write you another letter and keep our correspondence going. It was not an easy decision but after much thinking, I realized that there are still a lot of questions that I need to ask you. Also, I choose to keep talking to you because I truly believe that narrow-minded people such as yourself ought to be rebuked and confronted with truth. Do not take advantage of my kindness, however, for if you persist in your bigotry, I would have no other option than to recuse myself from responding to your letters.

I am frustrated—*you* are frustrating—but I chose not to give attention to subjects unworthy of my time and attention. I would, however, like to proceed to my next inquiry. What is your God's position on the inexorable advance of technology?

Be careful how you answer my questions this time, for you do not want to be the reason I cease to communicate with you and cease to consider you a strayed brother.

May your eyes be open to the ways of modern man.

The Proud Atheist.
Marawi

Tuesday, April 4, 1995
1517 Year Zero BCE Road
Paradise, God's Kingdom

Brother Marawi,

I am unmoved by the things you accuse me of and the names you call me; for truth does not care about opposition or insults—those names and insults have no power over me nor distress me because I am in heaven. I cannot help but relay the truth that is in me when you pose a question. If you turn your back to the pursuit of truth, I am certainly not responsible, for learning, by nature, requires dissent and divergence of views.

Now, allow me to respond to your inquiry regarding technology. The everlasting and all-knowing God existed before humans develop the concept of time, he created mankind out of dust of the earth, and gave him intellect among his creation—an intellectual capability that he endowed mankind with but man has been using it both for good and bad. Man displays his cognitive ability in creating cunning works and by being creative (often referred to as technology and innovation in the present time). From the first time the first man, Adam, walked upon the face of Earth, humans are permitted to have a cognitive faculty, unequaled by any other creature. They have used their brains to build dwellings, cities, temples, and farms. Unfortunately, mankind has also misused his intellectual ability. He has made idols, created weapons to slay his brethren, and altered God's creation. In fact, one of the reasons the Lord has limited the days of man is because of the misuse of his brain, and God has hidden the knowledge of deep things from him until the last days. From the dawn of civilization, mankind has been arrogant with the intellect that God bestowed upon him: he tried to reach heaven by building the Tower of Babel, and boasts in his weaponry and inventions; as he speaks in his heart: "God does not exist, and our invention shall defeat him even if he exists and decides to meddle with the affairs of men." Had boastful men read Psalms 2, Isaiah 66, or Psalms 110, they would have never challenged the Lord.

Dear brother, let me assure you that the Father, the Author of what you call technology, is the One who created man and gave him the ability to think and reason. The knowledge and wisdom of man that you boast in has never managed to: count the number of sands on the beach, the stars in heaven, reach God's domain, find the key to immortality, produce blood, or can count the number of hairs on your head—things that God can easily tell. In understanding the so-called inexorable advance of technology that you spoke of—a mere foolishness to the Lord as he can put an end to it at will—you must look into why he commanded man to keep his precepts. Before creation, God was aware that unless man sees himself as a transcendent being—and loves his brother as himself and the land God made him to be steward of—he would be bound to destroy himself. The technology you boast in is now being used to bring destruction to your kind, and it will do you well to come back to godly knowledge before self-destruction.

Indeed, humanity has rejected God's Son Jesus Christ and his commandment that people should love each other unconditionally as he, likewise, loves them. Consequently, man is getting creative day by day with new ways to murder his fellow brethren out of envy, power, lust for wealth, and utter hate; starting with Cain who brutally murdered his brother Abel with a rock, to subsequent generations who used arrows and spears as tools for slaughter, and your generation that employs guns and so-called weapons of mass destruction (WMDs) to commit fratricide. It has come to the Father's attention recently that the technology that you boast in has brought you to a point of no return: humanity has developed weapons that threaten its own annihilation as it vies against itself for power, preeminence, and wealth. Alas, the heart of man is not satisfied with the knowledge the Lord blessed him with, as he misuses it to harm his brethren: those who have the gift of medicine misuse it to formulate poisons and devise methods through which they can get rid of the unborn more effectively; scientists have used their knowledge to make breakthrough discoveries that revolutionized the lives of humans; however, the same scientists misuse technology and invent more creative and barbaric ways of war, especially WMDs. Scientists also attempt to disturb the order of God' creation through what they call genetic mutation.

Beloved Marawi, this is the epitome of knowledge without God that he warned humanity against, and the reason the Lord exposed the sinful, dark heart of man and his depravity. It's for this very reason that God sent his only begotten Son (Jesus Christ) to come and die on the cross so that man can turn away from his wickedness and embrace the grace of God in order to love his neighbor and brother as himself. From his servant Moses who he instructed on how to heal the children of Israel in the wilderness, to his servants Bezalel and Oholiab who built the Ark of the Covenant, God has sent man of godly knowledge and wisdom to solve the challenges confronting mankind, some of whom were never allowed to fulfill their mission because of the murderous practice of abortion. Human cries and complaints have reached up to God in heaven over the years. Consequently, he has sent doctors and scientists, who have collectively found cures to diverse maladies. However, humanity grows increasingly materialistic and would not be content with the things he created; therefore, the Lord sent them men of cunning work who invented all sorts of novelties: cell phones, skyscrapers, airplanes . . . It is good that man continuously strives to perfect the gift that he bestowed upon him, as long as he operates in reverence to God. Let he that has the gift of medicine strives to perfect it; let he who has the gift of music sing for the Lord's glory, let he that has the gift of invention perfect it, and let he whom God chose to spread his Word to his creatures who haven't receive Christ do likewise. Amen.

Your brother,
Marawi

Friday, May 5, 1995
1939 Bemba Road
Kamda, Earthly Domain

Greetings in the Name of Science and Atheism.

B rother Melchizedek, I am sorry for taking such a long time to respond to your latest letter. Work has been particularly time-consuming these last few weeks, and I was doing my research in order to refute your claims. I must say, however, that I am deeply displeased with the level of arrogance that your God has shown so far. He not only boasts about creating the universe and humans, but now you claim that he is the one who allows us, the mighty humans, to think and make technological discoveries and breakthroughs. This is perhaps the most baseless claim that I have encountered thus far in my conversation with you. You claim that it is because the revered entity foreknew man and his intentions that he limited man's days and the scope of his intelligence. Well, this assertion will soon be proven wrong because we (humans) are currently working on attaining immortality via advances in medicine and other means. Additionally, there appears to be nothing in this universe that will be beyond human understanding in a few years. Our astronauts and aerospace engineers have managed to send both manned and unmanned satellites and space shuttles to domains beyond the earth. If your God is real, I have no doubt that we will be able to reach his domain and conquer it in the next few decades.

You also overemphasize the perceived negative implications of technology. Whereas most people would agree that technology has been overwhelmingly a force for good, revolutionizing the lives of humans in a number of ways, you and your God do not see this. Perhaps, your God is nervous. Humans will outsmart him and prove to be gods ourselves. If it weren't for technology, I am uncertain if humans would still exist today. From the threats of diseases such as the bubonic plague, HIV-AIDS, and the devastating effect of overpopulation, humans have no other savior than technology itself. Moreover, you think our mighty scientists and inventors are mere fools in sight of your revered entity? You boast of his unequaled intelligence—an intelligence that is unattainable by humans. Well, as I have previously indicated, I strongly believe that human knowledge and under-standing have no boundary. We, the modern humans have evolved greatly from our forefathers the Neanderthals. Of course, then our cognitive faculty was limited, but today, especially with the advent of technological devices, there is no limitation to what the human mind can do. Mark my word: Our intelligence will soon surpass that of your supposed God.

On a different note, you justify the fictional Creator's opposition to the noble and crucial advances of technology by fostering the misconception that the heart of man is bound on doing evil. You made reference to our forefathers, who fought each other with primitive means: stones, sticks, spears, bows and arrows, and affirmed that we humans are getting increasingly creative with the ways we kill each other. In an attempt to emphasize your point, you made mention of guns and weapons of mass destruction that supposedly menace the continual existence of humans. Let me assure you that the improvement in weaponry has not been a force for evil but rather that of good: wars last a lot shorter and humans conduct wars in a more civilized manner. Additionally, the invention of modern weap-onry—especially nuclear weapons—has proven to be instrumental in the reduction of conflicts, since it serves as a deterrent. It also keeps global population in check, thus reducing the risk of overpopulation. Although weapons of mass destruction have been around for more than half a cen-tury, atomic bombs have only been used on two occasions: in Nagasaki and Hiroshima. Therefore, a logical conclusion is that you and your God are taking the situation out of proportion and context by affirming that without the love of Jesus Christ, humanity is on the verge of collapse. We need not the love of Jesus Christ since we have outstanding diplomatic channels such as the United Nations, the African Union, and multinational arbitration platforms such as the International Court of Justice, International Criminal Court, and World Trade Organization. These institutions have proven successful because they managed to preserve peace for much of the twentieth and twenty-first century.

You ascribed the great exploits of our scientists, doctors, and inventors to your God by claiming that he is the one who gave them knowledge and the ability to reason. This claim is nonsensical because there is no such thing as a divinely-given and orchestrated intelligence. Intellectual superiority is a product of two essential factors: genetic inheritance and the result of personal effort to achieve an exceptional ability. I am also in dismay and disbelief that you once again have the audacity to challenge the indispensability of abortion, and affirmed that several political, scientific, and social geniuses have been sent by God to find remedies to the plights of humanity but were prevented by the practice of abortion. First, there is no empirical evidence for this claim. Typically, women who resort to abortion are financially unstable and realize that they do not possess the financial means to take care of the child. Therefore, it is safe to assume that the vast majority of aborted babies will not grow up to be successful individuals. Moreover, specialties derived from personal interests and ends are ascribed to your God when you said that he is the one who preordained specialties (purpose), citing that some are gifted with the gift of medicine, others science and preaching. This assertion makes no sense because no one is born gifted or strong in a particular area. A combination of upbringing, culture, and personal development determine what one grows up to become. Accusing our great men of knowledge and asserting that some have used the same gift your so-called Creator blessed them with for evil ends—doctors making poison and scientists creating the atomic bomb—does not help either. This allegation is outrageous in the eyes of humanity's grandest intellectuals.

For the sake of highly intelligent and capable men, I demand your apology.

Talk to you later.
Marawi

Technology

Salutations in the Name of the Lord Jesus Christ.

I have been indeed pondering your criticism and concerns in my heart. I shall proceed to offer clarifications to my previous points and trust that the Holy Spirit will work in your heart to help you attain full understanding.

Dear friend, you accuse me of being arrogant and inconsiderate but in reality, you are the one who has displayed an incredible degree of arrogance in affirming that humans are infinitely intelligent and there is no limit in what they can do. You also assert that mankind is on the path to attain immortality. First of all, let me assure you that human intellect is limited. The notion that one day humans will be all-knowing and achieve immortality remains an illusion that reflects the pride of man. In fact, the first sin ever committed was due to this misconception; Satan beguiled Eve and promised her immortality and limitless knowledge if she would eat of the forbidden fruit.[1] The contrary turned out to be true: she died and did not have the knowledge of God.

You need to clarify what you mean by "technology has been overwhelmingly a force for good," and what is the point of underestimating the devastating consequences of technology without the fear of God. I posed a significant question regarding the proliferation of nuclear weapons and the sinister practice of certain scientists who use technology to alter the appearance and function of divinely ordained creatures and perform deplorable acts such as abortion. Nonetheless, I detect a double standard in your judgment and assertion because your central argument for the rejection of God the Father and Jesus Christ the Son revolves around your perceived notion that God is flawed, since in your estimation, he cannot put an end to evil and suffering. You never give credit to God for being the Creator of life, for saving his creation in dire situations, and all the things that work in life. When it comes to technology, however, you changed your perspective: now, you are considering its pros and cons. Why not do the same with God?

You are right in stating that human life has been transformed by technology. I did not assert that nothing positive can come out of technology. My point was that the advent of technology has been both a force for good

---

1. See Genesis 3: 4–5.

and a force for evil, especially when used for ungodly reasons. Have humans discovered remedies for dreadful diseases and improved their quality of life? They have certainly done both. My objection is directed at your assertion that technology is the only savior or hope of mankind. From the beginning, in the days when man did not make breakthrough discoveries, God was his best ally, providing all that he requires for life (rain to water his crops; the sun for warmth and light; the earth to lay down his head and cultivate, and animals for food and milk, among others). The Lord took care of Adam and Eve's needs and it is safe to say that he wanted mankind to be progressive with the knowledge he gave them. At first, man was able to build houses out of mud, and he used horses, donkeys, oxen, and camels as a means of transportation and cultivation. Progressively, however, God increased his knowledge and allowed him to cook bricks and build towns and use horse-drawn carts as a method of transportation. Then, man started to build cities and introduced automobiles as a way to move from point A to point B. This trend continues to the present time, as skyscrapers and airplanes replace their predecessors. The progression of man's intellect serves to illustrate the wonderful plan of God for humanity. He is a God of patience that entrusts his creation only with what it can bear at a time. Mr. Marawi, one can conclude that human intellectual ability will never surpass that of God, and attempts to downplay the devastating effects of technology (knowledge) without God is part of the problem. You have no idea how much more advanced God's kingdom is when it comes to what you referred to as technology—I am speaking as an objective witness of both domains.

Wars have indeed not been infrequent. In fact, since creation, your planet has not been at peace. The hatred of mankind, initiated by Cain who killed his brother Abel, has progressively become worse and worse, and presently the number of deaths in international and intranational conflicts surpasses that of the previous twenty centuries combined. Throughout the ages prophets have been cautioning man to turn away from evil, but he chooses to remain stiff-necked, thus putting himself on the path of a devastating conflict with unmatched casualties and repercussions. You referred to the tragedies in Hiroshima and Nagasaki to emphasize that weapons of mass destruction have been a tool of deterrence. How about poison gas in World War I? Weapons of mass destruction do not only include nuclear weapons. Biological weapons have been used more frequently now, and let me assure you that a world that does not fear God and has nearly fifteen thousand nuclear weapons at its disposal is simply not a safe and hopeful world. The unquenched greed and desire for power and wealth can set your world on a course of collision and destruction at any moment. This is particularly what is wrong with a godless world, for if your people fear God, they won't need to create WMDs as a deterrent, for the fear of God itself is a deterrent from every form of evil.[2]

You boast in the various institutions that mankind hopes will achieve lasting peace in a society that seeks to be purely secular and liberal. By doing this, you hope to eliminate the indispensable role that God plays in refraining humans from total self-annihilation. The diplomatic channels that you discussed, and the UN, ICJ, ICC, WTO, and their like are no novelty, and they have been attempted since antiquity. The Hittites, for example, tried diplomacy with the Egyptians, and the Greek city-states have done likewise—all to no avail. There were also supranational institutions meant to prevent war between naval and land superpowers, but none had an everlasting effect, because eventually, the wicked heart of man causes him to kill his brother. I can, therefore, assure you that only the love and the Spirit of God can restrain man from doing evil, and if your world still exists today, it is by the grace of God who retrains the wickedness of man and that of the devil until his appointed time outlined in the Book of Revelation.

I expect you not to agree with the fact that God is the source of the knowledge that materializes into what you called technology. You cited two important factors that in your estimation contribute to this providential intellectual ability—namely, genetics and educational background. Well, dear friend, genetics did not create itself, and like I previously said, before a human is formed and science can determine his genetic makeup, God already knows that individual. Although education is important, it is not a must since the Lord can elevate a human in any way he sees fit.

Further, you reaffirm your support for abortion and claim that there is no verifiable evidence supporting the fact that many brilliant individuals are sent to contribute to society but were turned away because of the practice of abortion. Dear friend, you need not look anywhere else to get your answer. Talk to those who escaped from the hands of the pro-choice movement at the last minute. Several have gone on to become doctors, lawyers, scientists, and preachers. Our friend, Njekaoussédé Ahijah Hezekiah narrowly escaped death as a baby thanks to the intervention of the godly nurse who risked her job in saving his life—just like the midwives did in Egypt to save Moses. Brother Hezekiah as you know grew up to be a Christian lawyer, a

2. See Proverbs 8:13; Job 28: 28.

prolific writer, and is now serving in the Senate, enacting bills to protect the rights of believers. Also, your assertion that a child needs a financially stable family to become successful is simply untrue. In an ideal world, every child should grow up with parents who can provide for his or her needs, but there are children from destitute families who go on to achieve great things. Brother Adoniram Dasnan Asa is a living example of this. In fact, children from poor families tend to have a higher academic success rate in many parts of the world. The bottom line is that God's plan for a person will materialize, regardless of that person's financial, emotional, and physical state, as long as he puts God first and fixes his eyes on his divine calling (purpose). I serve a mighty God who performs mighty miracles. He can surely bring anybody through anything.

Brother, may your desire to know the truth never die.

Melchizedek

10

Poverty and Global Turmoil

Sunday, May 21, 1995
1939 Bemba Road
Kamda, Earthly Domain

Greetings deluded friend.

I had the opportunity to read your response and I am still a nonbeliever. Frankly, you could have done a much better job in convincing me but missed your opportunity. What an utter failure on your part! I would briefly summarize my disagreement with the things you made mention of in the letter, and then proceed to ask the next line of deep questions that have been bothering me for quite a while.

You made me realize that I have indeed been overlooking the negative implications of technology. However, I disagree with the notion that technology is God-given and progressive in nature because of your God's will. Like most scientists, I believe that technological advances come from nothing other than research and human intellect. Your lack of consideration for the tremendous effort that humans have put forth to achieve peace is appalling. You have totally neglected the many benefits of diplomacy and international organizations, for they have successfully curtailed several interstate and intrastate conflicts over the course of the twentieth and twenty-first centuries. It is therefore unfair to dismiss them entirely. You also offered the pathetic and classic answer, alleging that abortion has killed those who were sent by your God to solve the plights of humanity. Until that is proven, it remains a mere theory.

The following are my next two questions for you: Why are nations with the highest rate of religiosity the poorest? In the wake of degenerating global unrest, what is the end game for mankind?

I look forward to receiving your response.

Marawi

Tuesday, May 30, 1995
1517 Year Zero BCE Road
Paradise, God's Kingdom

Laphia Marawi!

Poverty is a mundane term intended to elevate the status of the earthly rich whose riches will not last forever; for in heaven it's quite a different social order. In the eyes of God, all his children are equal. He does not differentiate between those who are considered beautiful or tender-eyed, rich or poor, black or white, tall or short, American citizen or Chadian citizen. God commands his children to desire to know him, love him, make him known, and accept the death of his Son on the cross in order to commune eternally with him in heaven. When you stated that there is a correlation between religiosity and poverty, you failed to take into consideration two critical factors. First, whether deliberate or accidental, you obviously did not realize that poverty and religiosity are human terms, and as the Creator of the universe, God has a unique way of looking at the affairs of men. Second, what do you mean by the term "religiosity?" I am assuming you are referring to the self-professed, often glory-seeking individuals who claim to be experts in the things of God in the keeping of rituals, and whose actions demonstrate that they have an illusion of self-righteousness vis-à-vis God. Being religious means absolutely nothing to God. What he looks for in men is a pure heart that is bound to serve him. Christianity is about a relationship—a vertical relationship with God—for religion implies rituals and self-righteousness, in short, man's attempt to reach God.

Many people look into certain parts of the world and reason that it is because of their allegiance to God that the populace is destitute. This is just untrue because the Lord is a God of love and justice and cannot be the cause of misery, pain, and injustice in the world. The reason, dear friend, is the contrary. The suffering of the so-called poor people is caused by man's alienation from God, for without the fear of God, the powerful oppress and dominate the weak, the intelligent exploit the moderate in intelligence, those with an elevated rank in society despise those at the lower echelon of society; most unfortunately, the wicked man who claims to be religious misuses the name of God to oppress those under his dominion. Listen, I am speaking of the God of justice who said, "One law shall be to him that is homeborn, and unto the stranger that sojourneth among you."[1] Moreover, your argument bears little credibility because poverty is not new—it has existed for thousands of years (it precedes Christianity), and societies that do not fear God also have poor and rich among them. Hinduism, for example, with its millions of gods and goddesses has an enforced cast system that determines the status of its adherents, without the opportunity for them to charter their future.

Some people make the mistake of correlating poverty with happiness and well-being—but this is not true. Many affluent nations today were at some point Christian nations and used biblical principles to prosper, accumulate wealth, and establish their governments and judicial system. Poverty, as commonly understood is obsolete because it is mainly a relative term. What do you mean by poverty? Are you referring to monetary accumulation? If so, different currencies are in use throughout the world, and just because you may have more money than a servant of God in India, for example, does not mean you are wealthier. Are you talking about poverty in terms of materialism? Well, once again, there is little correlation between one's income and happiness. In fact, quite the contrary is true: a lot more people who are monetarily and materially rich are unhappy compared with those who have less.

It is ironic that some people claim that the primary reason for their rejection of God is because of the seemingly unexplainable and widespread suffering and misery that humanity confronts: health, emotions, finances, and acceptance, for example. I, indeed, find it interesting that the atheist's excuse for not believing in God is because of the prevalence of evil in the world. The reality though, is actually the opposite: the so-called affluent nations in Europe and the Western hemisphere claim to have virtually everything they desire—stable government, considerable wealth, and ample opportunities for jobs and social mobility—yet they are the most atheistic, and in many

---

1. Exodus 12:49 (KJV).

cases want nothing to do with God. On the other hand, the countries that are regarded as less fortunate tend to have faith in God—those with limited resources and comfort are the closest to the Lord. Moreover, instead of directing the accusation at the Lord, humanity should do a self-reflection: the top 10 percent own 85 percent of the global wealth, leaving 15 percent for the bottom 90 percent; and the top 1 percent is on track to own two-thirds of global wealth by 2030. As you can see brother, it is easy to deny the depravity of man and his sin of greed and to blame God for the misery of his creatures, but being honest about the responsibility of man when it comes to suffering is a forgotten reality in your domain. Dear friend, people who might be considered poor in your world but have accepted Jesus Christ are a lot happier than their so-called wealthy, but lost, counterparts, for they have the assured promise of joy in heaven. Being rich does not mean having an abundance of perishable bank notes and goods that are destined to have a limited life cycle—true happiness and wealth are found in Jesus Christ. Wealth and comfort are dangerous for a child of God; for they may steal his heart and he will forget his maker. You are right, however, in your assertion that the true believer's first priority is not to accumulate wealth, although God can bless with wealth if he chooses to. Jesus instructed his followers to seek the kingdom of heaven first: "For whosoever will save his life shall lose it; but whosoever shall lose his life for my sake and the gospel's sake, the same shall save it. For what shall it profit a man, if he shall gain the whole world, and lose his own soul? Or what shall a man give in exchange for his soul? Whosoever therefore shall be ashamed of me and of my words in this adulterous and sinful generation; of him also shall the Son of man be ashamed, when he cometh in the glory of his Father with the holy angels."[2] In understanding the things of God and his estimation, you must not make the mistake of looking at the way humans judge, what they deem good or bad, wealthy or poor, beautiful or ugly. Over and over again throughout the narratives in the Bible, God has used individuals deemed destitute and of lower status by society to accomplish great wonders, and some he has elevated above those who regard themselves as part of the nobility. I advise you to consider the life of David and John the Baptist as examples.

Also, I am glad you asked the question regarding uncertainty in the global system. In fact, this is the principal reason why I am concerned about your soul and am trying my very best to convince you to turn to Jesus Christ, lest it be too late. Beloved Marawi, before tackling this important question

2. Matthew 6:33; Mark 8:35–38 (KJV).

that you posed, one thing is certain: Jesus Christ, the Son of God is coming soon! It would be profitable for you to read Matthew chapter 24 to the end of that particular chapter. In that passage, Jesus Christ speaks at length of things that would happen and hinting at his coming: massive tribulations, persecution of believers, wars and rumors of war, chaos and confusion. Even atheists, unbelievers, and pagans are now concerned about the condition of global affairs: the threat posed by weapons of mass destruction, terrorism, rumors of wars, warmongers preying on their weak counterparts, rivalry among the dominant powers to attain preeminence, and the proliferation of abnormal acts and practices that are becoming a part of the norm. I had a chat with Jesus Christ last week. I did not speak your name anywhere near him, but he is aware of your inquiries and told me to keep on answering your questions and never grow weary, for Christ encourages informed decisions that save lost souls. Dear brother Marawi, the Savior wants me to remind you that you are fearfully and wonderfully made in the image of the Father. You whom he knew in your preconception state: before you entered the world of the mortals and despise the Lord in your pride. Be assured he knew you before you are, loves you dearly, and longs to enrich your life but you must accept the invitation he extends. Look around and see what's happening in the world, and the fulfillment of prophecies Christ spoke of millennia ago in Israel. He is coming soon, and you cannot guarantee an additional second of your life. He is coming soon. Accept him today in order to spend eternity with him, lest you perish in your sin with the devil.

Thank you for your continued interest in learning about the love of God.

Blessings,
Melchizedek

Tuesday, June 6, 1995
1939 Bemba Road
Kamda, Earthly Domain

Melchizedek,

You have the nerve to underestimate the devastating impact of poverty on communities around the world. I am shocked! Poverty is not only a human term but a self-evident fact, and affirming that a certain imaginary

God does not make a distinction between the rich and poor certainly does not solve the issue. It's indeed dubious that you and your God are aware of the scope and ramifications of poverty on third-world countries, and this lack of understanding is part of the problem. If your God is truly omnipotent as you claim, why doesn't he put an end to poverty once and for all? Do you seriously think that people have the desire to entertain the notion of your imaginary God when they have no food to eat or the means to take care of their needs? No. No one would truly worship your God for the promise of a better hereafter, while suffering tremendously in this genuine existence. You also appear to resort to an appeal to the heart in addressing the correlation between religiosity and poverty. You affirm that Christianity is a condition of the heart, and poverty in the third world is largely caused by bad leadership—leaders who do not have the word of your God in them—because if they do, they would treat their fellow humans with dignity. My friend, though this sounds desirable, it remains a fiction of a distant utopia. The fact of the matter is religiosity and poverty go hand in hand, and humans are suffering. What a flawed argument you made in asserting that the fear or the act of worshiping your God brings about prosperity and equality rather than poverty. It is inconceivable to think that an imaginary so-called God of love can have a relationship with physical and genuine humans and transform their realities in life. Even if I grant you the benefit of the doubt and suppose that there are other factors that contribute to global poverty besides religiosity, the issue remains unresolved. Poverty is not something that can disappear overnight, and the only way that it can be eradicated is for people to stop wasting their time on an imaginary deity and take concrete measures to address their plights.

Further, you raised the point of poverty not being an indicator of happiness. Dear deluded friend, though certain deluded people advance this argument, I submit to you that one's happiness depends largely on one's income. The overwhelming majority of poor people live a miserable and discontent life. The only reason they express a certain degree of contentment is because they have been brainwashed by those who oppress them, promising them that they have hope in the afterlife. This is regrettable, and the idea that one should be satisfied with his destitute state for an imaginary afterlife certainly does not resonate with me. Moreover, you attempted to dispute the definition of poverty in asserting that monetary accumulation does not equate to wealth. Contrary to your disillusioned mind, that is exactly what being wealthy or rich is. In my part of the world, children are instructed from a young age to value money as the most important commodity that holds a chief position in their plans for life, because without it, life would be largely meaningless and harsh.

You took advantage of my question regarding instability in the global system to advance your primitive idea of a so-called savior. The reason I posed the question to start with is that a great many people, instead of looking for productive ways to resolve growing problems, fold their arms and in an attempt to justify their inaction, affirm that this is the way things are meant to be: an inexorable oncoming destruction of humanity. Such individuals, for the most part are religious, and think that for some reason a certain deity would destroy the world in its current form and take those who follow him to his celestial domain outside of our solar system. You expanded on your point by claiming that atheists and unbelievers are also concerned by the state of global affairs. Personally, I see no difference between atheists, theists, and unbelievers on the fundamental level—for they are all human. What sets those who reject your God apart is the fact that they possess a decent level of intellectual ability—thus are not easily swayed to follow a nonexistent deity. We (the nonbelievers), although we admit that an unprecedented conflict with an unprecedented aftermath hangs in the horizon, are taking concrete steps to avoid it instead of remaining hopeless.

The false and self-proclaimed prophet whom you call Jesus Christ made an unsuccessful attempt to turn my heart to swearing allegiance to him by claiming that he foreknew me and is coming back soon to gather the so-called elect to himself. Dear friend, inform this lowly man that I am not interested in being part of his fantasy. I fear nothing, let alone the imminent end of the world. I am confident that should such an event happen, all humans will have the same fate—that is death, and after that—oblivion.

Last, you claim that throughout the fictional history of your Bible, the entity you call God uses individuals of lower class or the destitute to accomplish his mighty works and elevates them to the highest echelon of society. Well dear friend, apart from your imagined reality, this assertion remains an illusion of grandeur—at least in the world I am living in. Melchizedek, wealth often correlates with political power, elevated social status, longevity, and relevance in society. The vast majority of successful individuals nowadays are people who have parents who are financially well established. Those parents ensure the success of their children by sending them to top-notch educational institutions. If they elect to pursue the path of entrepreneurship, they provide them with capital. I do not espouse the notion of a divinely orchestrated destiny that you are talking about, because I was born extremely poor and later my life was drastically changed for the better. The self-evident fact of hierarchical wealth is evident by looking at current trends in the world: prosperous and stable countries remain prosperous and stable, while the poor nations that are inevitably unstable remain poor and unstable, despite the foreign aid they receive yearly.

Brother Melchizedek, consider these words that I penned. I expect further clarifications on your failed attempt to respond to my inquiries in your next letter.

Salutations,
Marawi Njerabé

~

Wednesday, June 21, 1995
1517 Year Zero BCE Road
Paradise, God's Kingdom

Dear Marawi,

You posed an important question as to why God does not put an end to poverty once and for all. However, in your zeal to discredit God, you falsely accused me and God of underestimating the magnitude of poverty in certain nations that you call third world. Dear friend, let me assure you that God is aware of every plight of his creature, as evidenced by Jesus Christ when he lived in the flesh on earth and sympathized with the poor, including weeping at the tomb of Lazarus.[3] You forget one important factor: Jesus Christ, who was the essence of God on earth, lived modestly, indicating that material and monetary possessions are not the most important things in life. Why wouldn't God put an end to poverty once and for all? First, you are giving an order to a God that you consider fictional, let alone able to perform what is beyond human understanding. Second, let's suppose God puts an end to poverty today. The problem of poverty would remain unresolved because as long as the heart of man remains hardened and greedy, and he embarks on quests to accumulate power and wealth, what you call poverty will remain a reality—survival of the fittest, as you said. Third, God operates in his own time and will act in accordance with his divine

---

3. See John 11:35

knowledge and wisdom. Remember the principle of dispensation. As you can see beloved friend, the problem is not poverty but where the heart of man is vis-à-vis God and other men, for unless he loves his brothers as God commands him to, gives to charity and seeks the well-being of his brother, efforts to eradicate poverty will remain an unfruitful endeavor, for they address the symptoms, not the root cause. It is indeed easy to reject the idea that the answer to tackling the issue of poverty lies in the implications of God's teachings in the social and interactive aspects of human life, but to offer a viable counter-perspective is another thing. If you reject my premise then, I would assume that you can show me how the secularists have something better to offer. So far, their program has proven unsuccessful because human efforts to eradicate poverty have largely been a failure, despite the massive financial, material, and human resources that have been deployed throughout the world over time. To sum up my point, reconsider what I previously mentioned about sin and evil. Poverty, likewise, is a symptom of a much deeper problem, that is, evil and the sin of mankind vis-à-vis his Creator and brother. Remember also that though pain and suffering are bad because they are a result of sin and Satan's attacks, God uses them for the good of those who are his children or desire to know him; for they can lead to a closer walk and dependency on God and salvation.

You vehemently reject the point I made regarding the correlation between happiness and poverty, in asserting that one's level of income is certainly related to one's level of happiness and fulfillment. If this is the case then, you haven't addressed the main question that I posed in my previous letter, that is, Why are the vast majority of ungodly wealthy people dissatisfied with their lives? It is common at times for well-off individuals to turn to alcohol and drugs in a bid to cope with their social and personal problems and sometimes to commit suicide, often more frequently than among those who are considered poor. Affirming that the only reason poor people are happy is because they have been brainwashed does not explain this reality and goes against logic. Mr. Marawi, be assured that wealth is not the source of happiness. Rather communion with the Creator brings about a lasting happiness known as joy.

As for your human perspective on poverty, you are right in affirming that wealth often correlates with political power, elevated social status, longevity, and relevance in society. However, as I have previously stated, God has a unique way of at looking at each of his children. The Bible says that one of the indications that one may not be living in the will of God is when one's values result from the desire to acquire the riches of the world, thus becoming a friend of the world. "Ye adulterers and adulteresses, know ye not that the friendship of the world is enmity with God? whosoever therefore will be a friend of the world is the enemy of God."[4] Wealth, political power, longevity, and relevance in society may all be indicative of being a friend of the world. They are nothing but vanity to God. The Lord made King Solomon exceedingly wealthy in riches and political power, permitted Methuselah to live for nine hundred sixty-nine years, surpassing human estimations, and brought King David from humble beginnings to a leader that wielded much political power. These examples show that there are things more important than wealth, status in society, and life on Earth— you are rejecting the very source of those precious things: God.

It is the unquenchable desire of man to enrich himself that gives birth to corruption in the world, including in worship places. Self-professed prophets, ministers, and so-called apostles teach messages that deviate from what is written in the Bible: instead of focusing on the devastating and deadly impact of sin and the need of salvation, they preach to appease, please, and enlarge the size of their congregation. The level of corruption is appalling and seems to be getting worse. Preachers and self-proclaimed prophets reach people via television and other platforms, claiming that they possess unique formulas such as anointing oil, special healing power, and the ability to make one exceeding wealthy. They claim that they can pass on these false gifts and request victims to send money in order to buy their service. Although anyone who studies the Scripture would see this ploy and charlatanism, the hearts of pseudo-Christians in this generation are deviant from God to a point that they follow these sinners rather than sticking with God's revealed Word, the Bible, that teaches that there shall arise many false teachers in the last days to lead the fainthearted astray.[5] The gift of God is always free. If believers have doubts, they can check the Scriptures where Elijah healed Naaman the Syrian and refused to receive a gift in return, and the magician who wanted to buy the gift of healing from Paul but was rebuked[6] Be assured that individuals who claim to be servants of God but do not do his will and lead many souls to eternal damnation do not have the Spirit of God in them but rather that of the quest for wealth and desire to be accepted in society. Equally important, it is the duty of

4. James 4:4 (KJV).
5. See Matthew 24:24
6. See II Kings 5: 15–16; Acts 8:9–24

every believer to be cautious about who they follow and test their words (teachings) in light of the Scriptures. To do this effectively, believers must know this fact: Worshiping God does not guarantee financial and physical well-being in the present age. Although God most certainly has the ability to make his servants exceeding rich and healthy, this ought not to be the reason to worship him. Humans ought to worship God for who he is and not just for the rewards that he promised to those who follow him till the end of their lives.

You pointed out that your society raises children to cherish money and regard it as a chief element of their present and future happiness. If I were part of your society, I would be alarmed and deeply preoccupied with this fact, for any society that highly values money and materialism—especially the one that raises its future generation to do likewise—is certainly headed for destruction. Any society seeking to retain its moral and social incubus should focus on (1) the upbringing of godly children who can make a distinction between evil and good, values and vices; (2) the adoption of God as a point of reference in the way that society comports itself, and deals with others; and (3) a God-fearing judicial system, so that mischief and favoritism does not pervert the land.

Dear Marawi, you deride those who hold that the world in its current form is headed for destruction, and only the saved will be taken to be with the Father in heaven. Yet in your secular and atheistic paradigm you made an interesting observation by enquiring as to Planet Earth's fate in the wake of an increasingly turbulent global system. Unlike individuals such as yourself who have either never bothered to read the Bible, or read it with the preconceived mind of a cynic, the people whom you are underestimating as religious have a firm confirmation of the events happening in the world presently; thus, nothing surprises them. I highly recommend that you read the four Gospels in the New Testament and the Book of Revelation. I truly believe that it would change your perspective and how you view global events. What concrete steps have nonbelievers taken to address the troubles in the world? All your pride-driven efforts thus far have gone in vain, and the world is a lot more dangerous today than when your so-called institutions for peace were not institutionalized. Some of the multinational organizations that are meant to promote peace and equality are a platform used by the more powerful to oppress the poor and keep them in a permanent state of subjection. Believers are not uneducated and less important as you portray them to be. Contrary to your view about them, they are the wise and intelligent ones because they invest in their eternal future: they acknowledge that there is one God, refrain from sin, and accept the sacrificial price of the Lamb of God—Jesus Christ—on the cross.

It is a serious matter that you referred to Jesus Christ, the only begotten Son of God as a "lowly, uncivilized man who tells fantasies." I caution you dear friend, be mindful that you are speaking about the Savior whose coming and deeds were foretold by many prophets, including Isaiah who said: "Therefore the Lord himself shall give you a sign; Behold, a virgin shall conceive, and bear a son, and shall call his name Immanuel."[7] The name "Emmanuel" means "God with us." Therefore, any blasphemy uttered against Jesus Christ, as you have done in calling him a charlatan, is an offense to God, for the Father and Son are one. The Lord Jesus Christ heard the unkind words you spoke against him but holds nothing against you. On the contrary, he offers a standing invitation for you to become part of the Father's celestial domain—an adopted heir to eternal life. You are blinded by the prince of the world you live in, because you show the utmost arrogance and contempt in rejecting the Creator of Planet Earth who knew you before you were conceived in your mother's womb. Last, warning you about the imminent end of the world is not to instill fear in you but rather to warn you to be watchful and responsive to the call of mercy and grace. Your last day can arrive at any moment, and unless you are born again, as much as it would pain me, brother Marawi, you will spend eternity in hell—not just die and face the same fate—that is, according to you, eternal oblivion. God is a God of justice. He will not let the just and unjust face the same fate. The Bible states "And as it is appointed unto men once to die, but after this the judgment."[8] Be vigilant, invest wisely in your eternal future, for the time is near and will come abruptly, just like a robber who robs at any given moment.

I very much enjoy reading your inquiries and responding to them.

Of course, should you have further inquiries, do not hesitate to pose them in your next letter.

Your friend,
Melchizedek

7. Isaiah 7:14
8. Hebrews 9:27 (KJV).

Sunday, July 23, 1995
1939 Bemba Road
Kamda, Earthly Domain

Friend,

For the sake of this correspondence, I grant that you offered a legitimate answer regarding why your God—if he is as powerful as you say—does not put an end to poverty and suffering once and for all. Although I still believe that he is incapable of achieving such a daunting task, you remind me of the responsibility of mankind vis-à-vis poverty: we (humans) do need to be more caring toward one another, but one mustn't use this as an excuse to advance Christianity. Your claim that the destitute are considerably happier than their wealthy counterparts is nonsensical. Social problems such as depression, alcoholism, and suicide are present at every echelon of society—and not strictly limited to those with money. I cherish riches and would raise my children to do likewise—unlike you who advise people to put their faith in an imaginary God while confronting hunger and imminent financial disaster. You are overly pessimistic about the fate of our endeared planet. I posed the question of uncertainty, conceding that there is a certain level of uncertainty in the global system but you exaggerated my admission and took the question out of context: as usual, you seized the opportunity to advance the pathetic agenda of your God, asserting that there is "no salvation and hope for man except through Jesus Christ." Do not underestimate us humans. We have managed to resolve our differences peaceably for centuries without having recourse to your God. This too shall pass.

I categorically reject your Jesus Christ who is using the fantasy of hell to instill fear in me in an attempt to persuade me to get involved in the cult of personality. I wonder why you shared our correspondence with uninvited parties. I have no interest in adopting your values regarding the importance of wealth, power, and status in society, and refuse to be persuaded by the stories of a certain king named Solomon and the old man, Methuselah. In sum, your God is not the source of the things we discussed. Man is. Glory to man in the highest!

Dear friend, I leave you with this question. You can answer it in your next letter. Does your God prefer one race over another?

Thanks,
Marawi

11

Racism

Friday, August 11, 1995
1517 Year Zero BCE Road
Paradise, God's Kingdom

Greetings and Salutations,

Thank you for your continued interest in investigating the truth for yourself and the willingness to stay in touch, despite our divergent views and opinions on the most controversial topics of life.

Does your God prefer a particular race? No! Let me be clear and candid: there is only one race—the human race. This holds true for both creation and the destination of man's soul after death. Allow me to reiterate that God looks at the heart of man more than anything else; as he told prophet Samuel that he sees what's inside a man, unlike the appearance that humans behold.[1] The Bible in Genesis (regarding creation) does not embrace a particular group of people but rather humanity as a whole. The biblical account of creation reads thus: "And God said, Let us make man in our image, after our likeness: and let them have dominion over the fish of the sea, and over the fowl of the air, and over the cattle, and over all the earth, and over every creeping thing that creepeth upon the earth. So God created man in his own image, in the image of God created he him; male and female created he them. And God blessed them, and God said unto them, Be fruitful, and multiply, and replenish the earth, and subdue it: and

1. See I Samuel 16: 7.

have dominion over the fish of the sea, and over the fowl of the air, and over every living thing that moveth upon the earth."[2]

Dear friend, by reading this biblical narration of creation, two things stand out. The first is the supreme position that man takes in relation to all of God's creatures: he is made in the likeness of God, and has dominion over the animals, the vegetation, and the ground. Second, nowhere in this account can one find evidence of partiality or preference given to a particular race: the word race and skin color are not mentioned. The biblical position is simple, concise, and clear. What complicates the simple concept of creation is the fact that individuals with evil intention try to find ways to divide and undermine God's message by erroneously asserting that God is a partial God who holds a certain race in higher esteem.

Throughout the history of mankind, men have invented all kinds of presumed distinctive features in their appearance to advance self-centered motives. God, however, is extremely displeased with the concept of racial superiority. Indeed, the confusion started when humans started to identify and care only for their immediate family, tribesmen, and communal and regional groups. Soon thereafter, people began to refer to one another with terms such as oriental and occidental, autonomous and foreigner, black and white, Cameroonian and French, and so forth. These pseudo-differences then heavily influence and determine the manner and extent of interaction among people. Consequently, despicable practices such as slavery and the subjugation of particular communities took intercommunal and intracommunal dimensions, as one group of people seeks to gain the upper hand against another. Humanity has thus forgotten that in the beginning, God created man in his own image and that's all that matters. Factors such as the amount of pigmentation in skin, language, and place of habitation are secondary and should not be used to divide and put the children of God at conflict with one another.

Dear friend, you are not the only person who struggles with this question. In fact, prior to my passing, though I had friends from various cultural backgrounds, I often wondered whether God prefers a certain group of people. Being a native of a particular place, I resented the slave trade and believed that God loved a particular group of people more and gave them the upper hand on the rest of humanity. This belief was further exacerbated by the political and social climate that reinforced this false notion of partiality. Unfortunately, I resented hatred toward some of God's creatures.

2. Genesis 1:26–28 (KJV).

Thank God my heart was transformed by Jesus Christ. Now I realize that race doesn't matter, as I see people from all cultural backgrounds here in God's Kingdom: Tatars, Turkmens, Aztecs, Uzbeks, Incas, Sudanese, Polish, Taiwanese, and Batswana. We are all God's children, singing and glorifying God with the heavenly angels.

May your desire to seek the truth never be quenched by the Enemy. Have a great weekend!

Melchizedek

Monday, August 28, 1995
1939 Bemba Road
Kamda, Earthly Domain

Brotherly salutations,

I received your letter last night after work and need clarification on some of the assertions you made, chiefly that of the ambiguity surrounding racial identity. You assert that your God who is all-powerful and all-knowing, does not favor one race over another, and that the concept of racial identification is a human construct that has nothing to do with the Creator. If this is true, then why are some people considerably more well-off and privileged than others? I sometimes wonder whether there is something sinister behind the deplorable interracial cleavages. Individuals of a certain part of the world have been for centuries marginalized, bought and sold as slaves, have endured colonialism and neocolonialism, and account for much of the global population that lives in extreme poverty. If your God truly exists and is the champion of equality as you claim, why does he not put an end to social inequality along racial lines once and for all? While reflecting on this topic, I remember the comment of my friend Zimri Hawking who claims that Christianity is a religion designed to keep a certain group of people in bondage, while being exploited and their resources pillaged. Indeed, verses drawn from the discourses of your self-professed Messiah, namely the Sermon on the Mount, are used to keep oppressed people silent. Passages such as "blessed are the poor"[3] became instrumental in conquering the mind and eventually the land and resources of third-world countries.

3. See Luke 6: 20.

Moreover, I reject the notion that your God created man in his own image and does not make the distinction between the colors of the skin. You blame this reality fully on mankind, without realizing that they are the victims and not the perpetrators. No one in his right mind would assume that racism is a concept developed purely by men who seek to advance narcissistic ambitions.

When I was young, I had a neighbor who used to tell his children that Christianity was a foreign belief, and that his people were highly favored by God. He claimed that the Bible had been changed to reflect the desires of jealous individuals who used it to advance their plans and agenda throughout the world. I didn't object to the possibility that a supreme God existed at this point of my life, so I never took his claim into consideration. But now that I am trying to understand what motivates people to become Christian, I think there is some rationale and merit to this assertion—after all, religion has been used as a tool to enslave and colonize. Also, you did a mediocre job explaining what accounts for the seemingly everlasting racism around the world by implying that societies have been at conflict with one another for millennia and that the concept of racism is progressive in its spread. Granted this is true, it only explains part of the issue, because racism has been endemic with human history for thousands of years.

I expect further clarification from you as you attempt to defend the indefensible.

Marawi

Tuesday, September 12, 1995
1517 Year Zero BCE Road
Paradise, God's Kingdom

Greetings!

May this month bring prosperity and spiritual stability to your house in the name of Jesus Christ, the One who told his disciples: "Behold, we go up to Jerusalem; and the Son of man shall be betrayed unto the chief priests and unto the scribes, and they shall condemn him to death, And shall deliver him to the Gentiles to mock, and to scourge, and to crucify him: and the third day he shall rise again."[4] And so it was.

In your last letter, you stated that you believe that God does prefer a particular race over others because they are well-off and privileged. Your rebuttal has a number of flaws. First, the children of God are scattered throughout the face of the planet, therefore, which groups of people are you comparing? Second, the terms "well-off" and "privileged" do not mean much to God because that is not how he views his creatures. In God's eyes, all humans are created equal, regardless of their skin color, nationality, and temporary earthly riches. Third, if God is to be blamed for the hatred of men, then why do various societies that existed prior to Christianity (and those that are not Christian today) have traditional beliefs and cultures that, according to your definition, are racist? Fourth, if it is indeed true that Christianity is the reason for slavery, then why did the Roman Empire (pagan) have more than 70,000,000 slaves and the Arab slave trade was far worse in scope? The institution of slavery is without a doubt an illogical outworking of Christ's teachings, for Christ himself taught that there are only two kinds of people in the world: those who have accepted Jesus Christ and are thus saved, and those who have rejected Christ and are thus condemned. Never judge a worldview by its abuses but judge it by its pattern of conduct. Perhaps, you should consider why all humans face sickness and death? Is salvation available to all or a selected few? Injustice is injustice and does not have a color—whether intracommunal or extracommunal—it is an evil practice that God abhors. Let me remind you that as an atheist, you have no moral foundation to even raise the question of racism because according to your worldview, man is a result of random mutation (no better than dirt), with no intrinsic and objective value. Your morality is therefore subjective, and you only make the argument because beyond your rebellious heart, you know that you are created in the image of God; therefore, objective personhood, dignity, and truth exist. As for matters pertaining to slavery and imperialism, the name of Christ has been hijacked to carry out heinous acts. However, these acts in themselves do not invalidate Christianity because much of the emancipation and independence movements drew inspiration from the Word of God: equality of man before his maker, compassion and sympathy for the oppressed, and the concept of justice: these values are anchored and rooted in the teachings of Christ. Notable

4. Matthew 20: 18–19 (KJV).

Christians such as David Livingstone were also very vocal against slavery and actively freed slaves.

I would advise that instead of overstating your grievances, indicating that they are proof of the partiality of God, you ought to judge by the Word of God. Race and cultural background become irrelevant when the Scripture is the focus. What would constitute a cessation of inequality along racial lines as you claim? Is making everyone exceeding rich in money and possession—perishable things that would certainly steal their heart and lead them to eternal separateness from the Creator—the answer? There are poor and rich people in every community—it is a reality of the fallen world. The question that should be asked is, Why is there so much suffering and injustice in the world? And my friend, if you ask that question, you shall soon conclude that there is more responsibility of man vis-à-vis his challenges than he believes. It is easy to blame everything on God, but to do a self-evaluation (inward evaluation) is not desired by man.

You think Christianity is an invented religion by a particular group of individuals to suit their imperial needs. My friend, before voicing such blatant and erroneous allegations, it would be helpful to know the historical development of Christianity. It is a religion that was neither founded by man nor meant for a particular group of people. What is today referred to as Christianity started millennia ago when God appeared to a modest citizen of the land Ur in Mesopotamia named Abram. After heeding the instruction of the Lord to leave his kindred and move to the land of Canaan (modern Israel),[5] Abraham (Abram's new name given by the Almighty) begat Isaac in his old age. Isaac had Jacob as son, and Jacob and his sons immigrated to Egypt because of the great famine that ravaged the land of Canaan.[6] While in Egypt, that generation was treated well because of Joseph (Jacob's son who was sold as a slave to an Egyptian aristocrat named Potiphar but rose to prominence because of his integrity and ability to interpret dreams).[7] Following the subsequent generations and the death of the pharaoh who welcomed the children of Jacob (Israel), the Egyptians' attitude changed from hospitality to outright xenophobia and oppression.[8] The children of Israel became slaves, and after four hundred years in servitude, God kept his promise (covenant) of making Abraham's offspring great

5. See Genesis 12: 7.

6. See Genesis 46: 8–26

7. See Genesis 41; Genesis 47: 1–12

8. See Exodus 1: 8–16

and a people that would bring salvation to the rest of the world, by sending Moses, a mighty man of valor who performed awesome miracles, and eventually forced Pharaoh (the king of Egypt) to let the children of Israel go.[9] Subsequent to their exodus from Egypt, the children of Israel spent forty years in the wilderness en route to Canaan because of disobedience.[10] They had to defeat formidable kingdoms before finally gaining the upper hand and becoming the predominant community in the Levant. It was in this kingdom that many kings and prophets arose, the seal of whom is Jesus Christ whose followers became known today as Christians.

The Scriptures do not emphasize the skin color of the Jews but rather the fact that they are from the godly line of Shem (one of Noah's sons).[11] Furthermore, during the early days of Christianity, the good news (gospel) was preached to diverse people of different languages—from the valleys of the Middle East to the rugged terrain of Central Asia; from the distant frontiers of the Roman Empire to the Kingdom of Ethiopia and the highly polytheistic societies in the Indian subcontinent. History tells us that the apostle Philip preached in Asia and was led by the Spirit to the desert where he converted an Ethiopian eunuch whom Philip then baptized and took the good news with him back to Ethiopia.[12] Matthew preached in Ethiopia and Parthia. Mark preached in Alexandria, Egypt and Libya; Andrew spread the gospel in many Asiatic nations, including Greece where he met his death; Apostle Peter preached and met his death in Rome; Apostle Paul preached in Spain and Gaul and was eventually killed in Rome; Jude was a preacher in Persia where he became a martyr; Apostle Thomas converted many to Christianity in India and was thrust through with a spear there and died; Simon the Zealot preached with great success in Mauritania, other parts of Africa, and Britain where he encountered martyrdom.[13] Based on this list and the manner in which the apostles who walked with Jesus died, it is irrational to conclude that their message was geared toward a particular group of people. The people that you refer to as privileged and well-off also received the good news, although they were not the founders of the faith. From its onset, Christianity was never about race. It was about the depraved state of man in sin and the salvation plan of God to save man through the

9. See Exodus 12: 30–51

10. See Joshua 5:6

11. See Genesis 11:10–27

12. See Acts 8: 26–40.

13. See Acts 8: 26–40; Foxe's Book of Martyrs

death of his Son on the cross. Faith in Christ is the only remedy for man's desperation vis-à-vis sin.

Moreover, there is ample evidence for the universality of Christianity and its tolerance of all creatures of God in the Bible. Jesus resurrected the daughter of a Greek woman[14] and witnessed to a Samaritan damsel who accepted salvation along with many other Samaritans.[15] Jonah preached and warned the inhabitants of Nineveh who then repented.[16] Anyone who states that Christianity belongs to a particular group of people and uses this as a pretext to oppress his fellow man or accumulate financial gains and increase his political power is not of God but of the father of lies, the devil. Although the person in question may think that he is doing the Lord a service, he is actually doing him a disservice and does not have the Spirit of God, for he has the spirit of the ruler of your world who is Satan—the deceiver. You refuted my previous point about humanity being at conflict with itself for as long as Planet Earth existed, despite that this fact is plainly evident. Beware that what you refer to as racism is only a part of the problem. The seemingly eternal problem that man has is his rejection of the Creator and the unwillingness to see his fellow man as created in the image of the Creator. Sin abounds, and unless man sees himself the way God sees him and returns to the Word of God, there is no remedy for the disdain that one community shows toward another.

May the God who saved my soul bring you to his saving knowledge.

Melchizedek

Sunday, October 1, 1995
1939 Bemba Road
Kamda, Earthly Domain

Brother Melchizedek,

Thank you for sharing your objections to the points I raised. You have thus far shown a great deal of intellect and willingness to keep this correspondence going in spite of our conflicting views. Your answer

14. See Mark 7:24–30.

15. See John 4: 1–42.

16. See Jonah 3.

concerning divides among communities and the idea of partial privilege made me reexamine my stance on those issues. Although I disagree with most of the counterarguments offered because they are based on precepts derived from your imaginary God, I nonetheless got the opportunity to look at the issues from a different perspective.

What do you mean by saying, "God's children are scattered through-out the world." I would like to reiterate that there is no such thing as children of God scattered throughout the face of the earth because there is no God. The only scattering that I am aware of is that of evolution, with consensus among scientists that it originated in Africa. As for the privilege enjoyed by certain groups of society, it is an undeniable reality, although you tried to sugarcoat it and pretend that it does not exist. Apart from your imaginary utopia, there is no such thing as an egalitarian society, and racial inequality is a great grievance that must be addressed.

Moreover, dear friend, it is unnecessary to share the fictional story of your God. Your religion is a product of a recent imagination put forth by a particular group of people, and I am unconvinced otherwise. Abraham, Isaac, and Jacob are all imaginary characters invented by the crafters of the incoherent book that came to be known as the Holy Bible. In addition, you have an incredibly negative view of human nature. You stated that your cult called Christianity is not about race but rather a remedy for the desperation of mankind vis-à-vis sin. Unlike your imaginary and incoherent view, man is not desperate. He is an entity with a great deal of intellectual and physical capability; he is in no need of salvation. The word *desperation* denotes that there is no solution and hope. In the case of man, however, he is more than capable of tackling and resolving his problems, for he has made incredible strides in the area of medicine, science, and technology. To say that man is a desperate being is not only an offense to me but to humankind as a whole; humans should be the last of beings to be underestimated due to their higher degree of intellect and their ability to find solutions to their predicaments.

I concede, however, that humanity has been at conflict with itself since the inception of the universe. Indeed, our Neanderthal ancestors fought each other for various reasons: in certain cases, for the protection of their estates and families, but in other cases for sheer dominion of their neighbors and preeminence in their community. However, the scope and extent of the wars betwixt communities is not as overreaching as today. With the arrival of Christianity, however, the frequency of wars and conflicts mushroomed, for it came with devastating civil wars that devastated communities across the globe. These wars were a product of feuds and disagreement between Christian denominations. The trend continued when the ideology was exported to domains in Asia, the Middle East, Africa, and the Americas.

Unlike you, I subscribe to a different paradigm when it comes to racism: it is not merely a symptom of an underlying problem that you term *sin*. The concept of sin, let me reiterate, is one of the greatest lies invented to keep the human race in bondage. The term is broad and has a vague definition. We (the higher beings called humans who reject the myths and deceptions of Christianity) vehemently reject the notion of sin and refuse to be persuaded that all the injustices brought by your cult are simply a result of sin. The fundamental disagreement between you and me is that you look at social and political issues from the lense of religion, while I look at it from a scientific, verifiable paradigm. Having said that, it is not the belief in a Creator that will solve the plights of humanity, and neither will the lack of one perpetuate its suffering.

Your vague argument to criticize atheism is interesting, asserting that we—the highly intellectual atheists—have to borrow from theism every time we posit a moral criticism of Christianity. For you, there is no reference point in atheism to measure and determine what is good and honorable, bad and despicable. Mr. Melchizedek, you cannot be any more wrong than holding such a flawed view of atheism. We need no God because we are gods in our own right, instituting and encouraging virtuous behaviors and manners based on conscience and acceptable social precedence. We need no God to serve as a reference point for our moral decisions

Till next time.
Marawi

Tuesday, October 24, 1995
1517 Year Zero BCE Road
Paradise, God's Kingdom

My Dear Njerabé, Marawi.

May the God of grace show you mercy, give thee peace, and make his face shine upon thee. I thank the Lord daily for allowing us to be in touch, and share the spiritual progress that you are making with the host of angels in heaven. The angel Gabriel who has been carrying your notes to me in the afterlife and mine back to you is the same angel who appeared to Daniel and later to Mary, announcing that she would give birth to the Savior of the world, the One who would reconcile the godless Gentiles to the Father. Gabriel informed me that he very much enjoys being the middleman between you and me, and he commends you on maintaining this correspondence in spite of the apparent contradictory perspectives that we hold in regard to the deep questions of life: origin, meaning, morality, and destiny. In due time—when you come to recognize God as your heavenly Father and surrender your life to him, you shall meet Archangel Gabriel face to face.

Now concerning the things that you enquired of, it is true indeed that at one point in the history of mankind, Adam and Eve were the only humans placed in the garden of Eden. Shortly thereafter, the children of man (their descendants) built communities and villages located relatively on the peripheries of the garden of Eden. Then man rebelled by not scattering on the earth and attempted to erect the notorious Tower of Babel to reach heaven, thereby provoking the wrath of God who brought confusion upon humanity and dispersed them all over the face of the—earth. As you shall come to realize, there is no originality with Satan, for he is a thief who steals the things of God, including stories in the Bible and puts his own twist in them to conceal the counterfeit. The theory of evolution that you speak so much of is a ploy by Satan to sabotage the original and factual account of creation penned in the Bible.

It has never been my intention to defend a particular group of God's children, neither have I any desire to defend inequality in different communities. The point I raised was that what you call racial inequality has a profound root and is only one factor in a bigger equation. That problem is sin that hinders man from acknowledging that he is made in the image of God and seeing all humans as a community of brethren. As long as men keep separating themselves by creating ever-changing racial and geographic divisions, the issue of inequality shall never cease to exist. In fact, the desired utopia that humans have been longing for will never be achieved on earth: it exists exclusively in the kingdom of heaven and will come down during Christ's millennial reign.

Abraham, Isaac, and Jacob are not fictional characters, and Christianity is not a recent invention. In fact, your scientists are now uncovering many archeological artifacts and writings that yield undeniable proof that the Bible is true and has been indeed compiled over thousands of years. I encourage you to research the Dead Sea Scrolls, the tomb of Lazarus, the discovery of ancient biblical coins, the discovery Sodom and Gomorrah (with the highest concentration of sulfur on Earth, indicating that the city was destroyed in a fire), and tablets containing the name of King David, among others. These findings nullify the claim that the Bible is a piece of literature created in the post-Christ era. You claim that science is unbiased and objective, but the amount of dishonesty that contemporary science shows toward the Bible and the amount of effort pseudoscientists put in to hide irrefutable findings that validate the Bible is beyond words. Show me another book written by forty authors over a period of 1,600 years, all pointing to the same Savior (Jesus Christ), that is coherent, scientifically verifiable, and has stood the test of time and man's effort to eradicate it, and then you can refute the Bible. The Bible itself is indeed a living miracle and has been the most influential book in the history of mankind. It is the only book that comes with its author, the Holy Spirit, and every time an honest seeker of truth reads it, he can learn a new truth concerning life and God.

Dear friend, man is indeed desperate and in need of salvation. You keep reiterating that human understanding and intellect surpass all other creatures, yet when examined, humans make decisions that are far more foolish than that of animals. For instance, animals upon birth know their gender and their role in the family. Humans, on the other hand, through sheer dishonesty and pseudoscientific lies, claim that they are confused about their gender and come up with all sorts of names to describe their evil-driven beliefs. This example, among others goes to show how desper- ate and confused mankind truly is. It is the arrogant attitude of man that perpetuates his desperation and hinders him from accepting the remedy to his predicaments, that is, to humble himself and look up to the Savior.

Your argument that inter—and intracommunal conflicts have mush- roomed with the arrival of Christianity is unsupported. Any war that is supposedly fought in the name of Christ is fabricated by narcissistic in- dividuals and Satan himself because it is contrary to the marching order that Jesus gave his disciples—specifically, they are commanded to love one another and spread the gospel peaceably. Have you considered how many people are killed in the name of atheism, other religions, and ideologies? In fact, more people are killed in the name of atheism than any other belief system (with an estimated total greater than 100 million). Crimes commit- ted in the name of Christianity are different from others because they are a result of an illogical outworking of Christ's teachings. Crimes committed in the name of atheism and other ideologies are the logical outworking of atheism and those beliefs. Because the founders of those beliefs condone the atrocities and there is no point of reference for morality in atheism, morality is exclusively subjectivized.

Sin is not merely a broad and vague term, but a fundamental problem that each and every human being deals with. Sin is the state induced by Adam and Eve by their rebellion; hence every human is a sinner, and sin is manifested in actions and/or words that one utters knowingly or unknowingly that are contrary to the precepts of God the Creator. In essence, it is the result of one's action despite the quiet inner voice of conscience and of the Holy Spirit, whispering quietly—yet powerfully—that it is an offense against God. You and I do look at issues through different lenses. I rely on the Lord to give me understanding and answers to your inquiries. You, on the other hand, put your trust in the word of haughty and arrogant men who think that they know it all but in reality, know nothing. Conscience, which you claim to have, is God-given and metaphysical in nature.

It is indeed interesting that you stated that unbelievers are gods themselves to support your argument that the indispensable position of God as a reference point is unnecessary. You also argued that the triune nature of God constitutes polytheism. Yet you claim that everyone is a god? Are we dealing with multiple deities? Human nature is flawed and susceptible to sin, and man serving as his own point of reference based on conscience is highly problematic and dangerous. In fact, this is the main reason why the domain you abide in is plighted by all sorts of evil and is heading toward utter destruction.

Cordially,
Melchizedek

12

The Unreached, Leadership
in the Church, and Denominations

Friday, November 3, 1995
1939 Bemba Road
Kamda, Earthly Domain

Brother Melchizedek,

I had the dubious pleasure of receiving and reading your last letter. You twisted and changed my words to make it fit in your preconceived and brainwashed mind. I seriously feel sorry for you. What a pitiful soul!

What makes you think that I need to hear more about fictitious characters? You introduced a certain archangel named Gabriel who is supposedly the middleman between you and I. Tell this unknown character that I have no interest in meeting him and that he should focus more on entertaining disillusioned individuals like you.

I categorically reject your continuous belief in the myth of a certain garden of Eden. Please stop forcing your foolishness on me! Adam and Eve never existed and Abraham, Isaac, and Jacob are indeed invented character, regardless of your position. I believe in a different paradigm when it comes to how the universe came to be and how the concept of religion developed—nothing will persuade me otherwise.

As usual, you downplayed the point I made that man is not desperate but mighty in intellect and deed. You instead misrepresented facts to a point that you claim that many more people were killed in the name of atheism than religion. How can this be true? Most educated individuals and researcher would agree with me that it is religion that brings havoc in our world and not atheism. How dare you misrepresent atheism!

My last point of difference arises from the fact that you claim that I am promoting multiple deities by claiming that humans do not need God since they are gods themselves. My intention in raising this point is to rightfully elevate man to his rightful place and achieve much more for himself—not to promote fictitious ideas. If you are to reproach me, it would be better for you to look for a better thing to bring up.

Since you continue to challenge me, I have a question for you: What is the fate of those who died, having never heard of your so-called gospel?

Bye.
Marawi

Thursday, November 23, 1995
1517 Year Zero BCE Road
Paradise, God's Kingdom

Marawi,

You have done well in inquiring about the fate of those who died, having never heard the gospel, or who will die before the coming of Jesus Christ. This is a question that bothered me tremendously when I lived on Earth. It only deepened after I became a Christian, as I would frequently pray to God, asking him what is the fate of my brothers who died, not having the opportunity to receive Jesus Christ as their personal savior. The first mistake was that I assumed that I was God, therefore all-knowing. The question itself follows the assumption that the questioner is certain that certain people have never heard the gospel preached to them. This assumption has two fundamental flaws—namely, no one can be certain that the Lord has never convicted a lost soul about the need of salvation; it is an individual and subjective experience. Secondly, given the ever-increasing globalization and interaction among people—a clash of civilizations—it is becoming highly unlikely that a person has not heard of the name of the Savior Jesus Christ. Remember also that man had the true pathway to God in the beginning but decided to rebel, built the Tower of Babel, and rejected the Lord even after he destroyed the previous sinful civilization in the great flood. If anything, the blame falls on man, not God, for he chose to follow his heart instead of obeying the precepts of the Creator. God is indeed all-knowing, and his wisdom is beyond human comprehension; therefore, one cannot make assumptions and take his position as the supreme Judge.

Even those who do not believe in the Creator evoke this question, hoping that it would destroy the good news of Jesus Christ. The question itself would self-destruct and be meaningless if God did not exist and Jesus Christ did not die on the cross. What is certain, however, is that the concept of a unique and sovereign Creator is known throughout the world, and the innate desire to know him is also present in various corners of the globe. Various people on Earth came to realize the existence of God and have given him diverse names, though their conception is often distorted. Now, the problem is that the heart of man is bound on doing evil; therefore, he typically chooses to align himself with Satan, going after other gods and rejecting the call of God for fellowship. One thing should not be forgotten: it is appointed for man to die once, and after death, judgment.[1] All humans then, be they nominally Christian, Buddhist, Hindu, atheist, Pagan, or irreligious, will face God in the final judgment. In the final judgment, no one can decide the fate of a soul apart from God the Father. This, of course, does not nullify the death of his Son on the cross (for he is the only way to the Father).Only God holds the last word and can decide who has or has never heard the gospel—it's not our job. The Old Testament, however, gives us clues about the fate of those who died prior to Christ's coming: animal sacrifice was offered to symbolize the coming Messiah who would shed his blood and in whom they must put their faith for salvation.

I hope I answered your question effectively. If further clarification is needed, mention them in your next letter.

Have a blessed week.

Your brother, Melchizedek

---

1. See Hebrews 9:27.

Monday, December 11, 1995
1939 Bemba Road
Kamda, Earthly Domain

Melchizedek,

I want to inform you that you did not offer a satisfactory answer to my question regarding the fate of those who died without ever hearing your so-called gospel or of a singular, supreme God. Your tacit concession that ultimately the final word rests with your God is unsatisfactory. As a nonbeliever, I would much rather believe in a god who allows people into his kingdom based on their work or the supposed fact that they are created by him. It is hard for me to imagine that all the people who died prior to Christianity—and those who are atheist, Buddhist, Hindu, and Muslim, among others,—would all end up in hell. We are talking about hundreds of millions of people here. This is a serious matter with tremendous magnitude.

I am amazed that you, the committed Christian with a tremendous amount of zeal, also struggled with this question. I thought that Christians were narcissistic people who are only concerned about themselves, both now and in the hereafter. I dismiss your statement that part of the problem is because people appropriate the prerogative of your God to them and think they have all the answers. In making this statement, you implied that since human knowledge is limited, they should not try to understand the flaws in the idea of needing Jesus Christ in order to preserve their soul from eternal damnation. I am not a fan of this suggestion because it is truly critical for humans to know the exact destination of our postmortem body. The fact that there is no clarification regarding this critical question proves that your God is selective in choosing who enters his domain. You wrongly affirmed that the question would be meaningless if the concept of a unique, sovereign God is taken out of the equation. We scientists believe that man is a material being, and after death, the body disintegrates and goes into the state of nothingness. I think the question does not self-destruct because you are the one who posited a moral and just God who judges the deeds of his creation. If this is the premise then, shouldn't everyone have an equal chance of going to that kingdom?

Further, your argument that virtually every culture has the notion of a singular God also fails when confronted with evidence, because the concept of a unique God is a modern concept that is a direct product of

Christianity. Spirituality during antiquity consisted of the veneration of multiple deities.

Last, I have an additional question for you: What's your God's position on leadership in the church and denominations?

I wish to finish my letter on these notes. I expect a speedy response to the well-grounded counterarguments that I offered in this letter.

Bye!
Marawi Njerabé

Sunday, December 25, 1995
1517 Year Zero BCE Road
Paradise, God's Kingdom

Dear Marawi,

E veryone does have an equal opportunity of going to heaven: Salvation is found in no other name but the name of Jesus Christ. You advocate a free pass to Heaven, assuming that if God created man and loves him then everyone should make it to Heaven. In such a paradigm Heaven wouldn't be Heaven because it will be full of unconfessed sin and all manner of filth of man that can only be atoned for by the blood of the Lamb Jesus Christ. God wouldn't be God because sin and filth would be ignored. Keep in mind that God's nature requires holiness and justice, and he cannot operate contrary to his attributes. Salvation is a gift, not a reward.[2] Rewards are earned, but Jesus Christ saved those who cannot earn their way to heaven.[3] You further show hypocrisy in your analysis because you raised a serious question about the existence of evil and the Christians who use Christianity to fulfill self-centered ambitions. My response was that work by itself is never enough to convince God to admit one into his domain. What is necessary is the confession of one's sin[4], acceptance of Jesus Christ as the only way to the Father[5]—and naturally a turning away (divorce) from sin—in order to be with the Father. If you take God out of the equation, the question

2. See Ephesians 2:8.
3. See Acts 4: 10–12.
4. See I John 1: 9.
5. John 14:6.

becomes even more meaningless because the good people would not get rewarded, and the bad people would not get punished. You have fallen into the dilemma of many atheists who judge the Christian God for upholding and not upholding justice. For them, they complain about the objective existence of evil men such as Hitler—that logically merit punishment, even by secular standards—but condemn the Lord when such men reap what they sow. Thus, the atheist dilemma and a proof of what the book of Romans referred to as "professing themselves to be wise, they became fools."[6] Those you refer to as evil men, God appointed a final judgment for such men, whereby justice will be rendered in his divine and unmatched wisdom. Yet, atheists complain when God upholds justice, claiming that no good God would send souls to hell. They are disillusioned by their own contradictions and seem to be confused about the concept of justice.

Further, I never claimed that Christians are immune to doubt or questions. In fact, like other mortals, every Christian has low points in life. The low points often result from tragic events during which the person finds it difficult to stand by the Word of God that says: "And we know that all things work together for good to them that love God, to them who are the called according to his purpose."[7] Thus, anxiety and uncertainty gain entrance in their mind.

Regarding those who've never heard about the gospel, consider what Paul said: "For as many as have sinned without the law shall also perish without the law: and as many as have sinned in the law shall be judged by the law; (For not the hearers of the law are just before God, but the doers of the law shall be justified. For when the Gentiles, which have not the law, do by nature the things contained in the law, these, having not the law, are a law unto themselves: Which shew the work of the law written in their hearts, their conscience also bearing witness, and their thoughts the mean while accusing or else excusing one another)."[8] Paul is also the same apostle that stood in the midst of pagans in Acts 17 and gave a discourse about how he marveled about the religiosity of the Athenians and their undying desire to discover truth, even dedicating an idol to the UNKNOWN GOD. Although Paul seized this occasion to share the gospel, asserting that the UNKNOWN GOD that the pagans were looking for is the only God who made the universe and everything therein, the majority of the pagans made

6. Romans 1: 22.

7. Romans 8:28 (KJV).

8. Romans 2: 12–15 (KJV).

a mockery of his words and chose to remain deprived, with no hope.[9] In fact, whether people lived before or after the incarnation of the Son (Jesus Christ), it is faith in God that saves them—not work or their own merit. Romans 1 shows us that man is without excuse when it comes to knowing his maker.

Furthermore, you accused me of encouraging blind faith and downplaying the supposed fact that according to Christian doctrine, people should be okay with not being certain with what will become of their earthly life and body when they die. This is a clear distortion of my statement because I answered both questions, but your cynical mind is unreceptive. God guaranteed salvation and eternal life for the soul who seeks him, and Jesus Christ rose from the dead to validate it. You are a perfect example of someone with a reprobate mind. God has made himself known to you yet you reject him. If Jesus were to come back to Earth today and perform miracles, many would still reject him. The problem is man's rebellious heart—not a lack of God's revelation. This is particularly what sets Christianity apart from other religions: assured salvation through faith in Jesus Christ instead of gambling on eternity based on good works. In short, Christians place their hope in a living a Savior—not a deceased prophet. Logic would dictate that if one were to place his faith in a person who speaks authoritatively about afterlife, he should listen to the one who was in the grave but conquered death three days later. A truly saved person cannot live perpetually in sin without a sense of guilt and a desire to make things right with God, for like any good father, the Lord will chastise his lost son or daughter and bring him or her back to the right path.[10]

What I find incredible is that you turned your questions around and accused me of turning over the table and positing a moral and just God. Your questions throughout the duration of this correspondence—whether or not posed deliberately—contain moral elements. You asked, How can a moral and just God send people who never heard the gospel or who preceded Jesus Christ to hell? This question, from an atheistic paradigm is meaningless because it has a moral nuance and deals with metaphysics—something atheism lacks and a luxury it cannot afford to have. In your worldview, glory is given to the individual and he is encouraged to do as he wishes. Given such a framework, with no objective reference point, why is it unacceptable or morally wrong for God to allow whoever he wishes into

9. Acts 17: 16–32.

10. Hebrews 12: 6–7; Proverbs 3: 12.

his heaven and set his own standards (conditions)? It is undeniable that meaningful, objective judgment of atheism requires borrowing from theism. The fact that you repeatedly assert from your worldview that—man is a material being that has no other value besides his physical state—already disqualifies you from making allegations about God and his supposed partial method of accepting people into his domain. If humans are nothing but animals with no soul, and God is an imaginary concept, then it is irrelevant to ask who and how people go to heaven. The ultimate decision regarding those who have never have the opportunity to hear about the gospel and the God of Bible rests with the Lord who will do that which is right and just. Who are we to argue over what should or will happen to the creatures created by God? Salvation has always been about man putting his trust in God—not man earning his way to heaven by his own merits.

As for your question concerning leadership in the church and denominations, examine the words of the Apostle John: "BELOVED, believe not every spirit, but try the spirits whether they are of God: because many false prophets are gone out into the world. Hereby know ye the Spirit of God: Every spirit that confesseth that Jesus Christ is come in the flesh is of God: And every spirit that confesseth not that Jesus Christ is come in the flesh is not of God: and this is that spirit of antichrist, whereof ye have heard that it should come; and even now already is it in the world."[11] The only intermediary of God on earth was, is, and shall be Jesus Christ who lived a holy, blameless life and offered his life as a sacrifice for the redemption of sin. Although there are servants of God throughout the world laboring for the propagation of the gospel and the kingdom of God, they are servants, not substitutes. Jesus Christ is Alpha and Omega, The Beginning and The End[12] established throughout the Scriptures. The Bible says that every man is a sinner and needs the forgiveness of God. In light of this declaration, no man is sinless or infallible: "For all have sinned, and come short of the glory of God."[13] The Lord Jesus Christ asserted that there is none good but God[14], and man by nature is inclined to committing error (fallible). This discussion goes back to my early argument concerning the necessity of a personal relationship with God the Father through Jesus Christ the Son. You see, beloved Marawi, Christianity is not about rituals, social structure,

11. I John 4: 1–3 (KJV).

12. See Revelation 21:6; 22:13

13. Romans 3:23 (KJV).

14. See Mark 10:18

or the veneration of a certain man that appropriates authority to himself in order to be equal with God. The Bible openly rebukes self-conceited individuals and warns Christians to know them by their fruits.[15]

Some people assert that certain men are and can take the position of an apostle and be representatives of God on earth, though biblically, an apostle must have physically seen the Savior. Jesus Christ clearly stated that he is the last prophet and his coming sealed the advent of prophets. He, however, warned believers that many false prophets would claim to come in the name of God, and assert that they represent the continuation of Christ's ministry on earth, but are in reality wolves in sheep's clothing. John explained this in 2 John 1:7: "For many deceivers are entered into the world, who confess not that Jesus Christ is come in the flesh. This is a deceiver and an antichrist." Rest assured, for God is aware of some of the outrageous heresies coming out of the headquarters of teachers of lies disguised as men of God: the denial of the reality of hell, the nullification of Christ's death on the cross and its sufficiency for salvation, the veneration of other personalities that takes attention from the true savior (Jesus Christ), the emphasis of tradition rather than the need to have a personal relationship with God, the questioning of the authority and reliability of Scripture, the denial of Christ's deity, and the lie that Jesus Christ was a mere good man and one among several prophets rather than the seal of the prophetic (direct) dispensation. As King Solomon stated, "There is nothing new under the sun,"[16] and these heresies are not new phenomena but existed in the time of the apostles as well. Apostle Paul wrote extensively in his epistles, especially to the Corinthians to address them. Apostle Jude also did likewise in his epistle. Any religious leader who does not see himself as a sinner and teaches a message contrary to the Word of God in the Bible is delusional and must be exposed, for such are wolves in sheep's clothing. Notwithstanding they can find salvation in the Lord as Christ said, "They that are whole have no need of the physician, but they that are sick: I came not to call the righteous, but sinners to repentance."[17]

I look forward to hearing from you.

Melchizedek

---

15. See Proverbs 29: 23; Matthew 23: 12; Matthew 7: 15–20.
16. See Ecclesiastes 1:9.
17. Mark 2:17 (KJV).

Saturday, January 13, 1996
1939 Bemba Road
Kamda, Earthly Domain

Dear friend,

Y ou criticize me for stating that a good, honorable God would not create an extreme form of punishment such as hell. In supporting that claim, you stated that the Christian God is criticized whether he upholds or does not uphold justice. I think you missed the whole point of my argument because I was not explicitly referring to the upholding or disregarding of justice. My simple point was that a good God would never send people to a despicable place such as hell. You did raise an important point in claiming that those who do not believe in your God have to deal with difficult questions: How can evil, guilty men be punished after death, and how can just, honorable, and virtuous men be rewarded when they pass away? Don't Christians who are following God also doubt sometimes and have questions regarding the God that they speak of and fervently try to share with others?

You have the audacity to question the authority of church leaders and different denominations, and this is a senseless stance and an utter disregard to the feeling of millions of people around the globe. Be assured that unlike your narrow-minded God, some leaders in the church and certain denominations are becoming our ally when it comes to same-sex marriage, interconfessional dialogue and coexistence, and the supremacy of scientific theories over theological paradigm.

Moreover, you have the nerve to state that highly revered leaders of other faiths, like other humans, ought to be judged by their fruit rather than status and position. In making this statement, you show a lack of respect for the position of founders of other faiths. Given that there are clearly some irreconcilable differences between certain leaders and what Jesus of Nazareth taught in the Bible, based on your previous statements, are you telling me that the words of Jesus Christ which were written down centuries ago supersede that of more recent religious leaders?

Besides, you spoke of the self-proclaimed prophet Jesus Christ as the seal of the prophetic age, meaning that your God no longer sends envoys to represent him on this planet after Christ. Thus all subsequent religious leaders who aspire for the position and qualities of your God and Jesus Christ—and have attained the presumed noble virtues—are outcasts who do not have the Spirit of your God in them. This is utter nonsense. All religions are a fabrication to manipulate gullible individuals for the intent of extracting certain interest from them. There is no objective validity in what you are claiming. As if your uncaring condemnation is not enough, you referred to those who disagree with your religious doctrine as "wolves in sheep's clothing." Well, my question is, how can one tell whether a person is an authentic follower of your God or a wolf in sheep's clothing? Your statement is the epitome of the confusion that arises not only between religions but also within them.

Last, your arrogance goes as far as attacking the core doctrines of other faiths, in opposing the notion of allegorical hell, the veneration of other personalities, and the so-called de-emphasis of a personal relationship with Jesus Christ because of tradition, as you have preached since the start of our correspondence. I did not have much knowledge about the concerned beliefs prior to reading your objections, since I prefer to stay away from anything that deals with the concept of God. However, after your senseless and insensitive comments, I have spoken with friends of other faiths and have done some research on their belief. Although I am not claiming to be a believer myself, the notion of an allegorical hell that is not determined by one's faith in Christ is logical. If someone believes in a benevolent God that created humanity, then the notion of eternal damnation, that is, hell is inconceivable. Although fictional, it makes sense that a temporal place of punishment would replace eternal punishment. What do you mean by traditions? Are you referring to rituals that may not be in line with your preconceived notion of worship? If so, what are the proper ways? As far as I am concerned, all religious traditions are the same: garbage!

Such are my observations. Reply at your convenience.

Marawi

~

Wednesday, January 31, 1996
1517 Year Zero BCE Road
Paradise, God's Kingdom

Brother Marawi,

I disagree with your position. I do have the right to criticize self-proclaimed leaders who elevate themselves above God, and I am not insensitive to the feeling of many followers of those men. My position does not change, and God Almighty, as I indicated bows down to no one, is co-equal with none, and is accountable to no one. All men are alike in that they are sinful and must submit themselves to the authority of God and the words penned in the Bible. This is not just my position, but God's position as well; therefore, it shall not change because of heretic teachings coming from humans.

Contrary to popular belief, not all religions, faiths, and beliefs are the same. They are fundamentally different and at best superficially similar.[18] I have, therefore, one thing to say concerning your position: God Almighty and his Word do not care about confused feelings but the preservation of truth. The Lord is infinite in his wisdom and dictates what is right and wrong with absolute, unhindered independence, and has prescribed the way of life in the Bible; therefore, humans must submit to his will—not the other way around. The Scriptures instruct that all humans are sinners and that ultimately the Word of God is paramount in all matters. Accordingly, anyone who believes that he is above criticism and beyond reproach is delusional since God is not a respecter of person—whoever speaks about something that is not in line with the Bible must be corrected since the Word of God is the supreme measure.

Also, your argument is baseless and futile even if God does not exist, for logic dictates that before religious leadership, the object of worship has to exist and connect with its subjects. In your letter, you also praised self-righteous leaders for being tolerant toward ungodly practices such as same-sex marriage, abortion, and the trumping of Christian values by scientific theories. If those are the reasons why you applaud some of these men and seek to elevate them above the Word of God, then such persons are not of God but of the world. The Word of God says that friendship with the world is enmity with God.[19] The Lord is not bound by anything or anyone,[20] and making yourself believe that certain men are infallible and God ought to accept their words and actions is a terrible illusion. All humans are accountable to God Almighty, but he is accountable to no one, as he told Abraham: "By myself have I sworn, saith the LORD, for because though hast done this thing, and hast not withheld thy son, thine only son."[21]

---

18. Ravi Zacharias
19. James 4:4.
20. Hebrews 6:13.
21. Genesis 22: 16.

Furthermore, it is a grave mistake to assume that since there is dissonance between the Word of God and that of certain religious leaders—coupled with the fact that Jesus' teachings were compiled centuries ago—whatever other leaders say should trump Jesus Christ's teachings. My dear brother Marawi, let me remind you that the teachings of Jesus Christ are more relevant today than when they were recorded, and if anyone challenges his teachings by teaching contrary doctrine, regardless of that person's status, he must be exposed and rejected as a fake prophet (messenger). Christ made this abundantly clear: "Beware of false prophets, which come to you in sheep's clothing, but inwardly they are ravening wolves. Ye shall know them by the fruits. Do men gather grapes of thorns, or figs of thistles? Not every one that saith unto me, Lord, Lord, shall enter into the kingdom of heaven; but he that doeth the will of my Father which is in heaven. Many will say to me in that day, Lord, Lord, have we not prophesied in thy name? and in thy name have cast out devils? and in thy name done many wonderful works? And then will I profess unto them, I never knew you: depart from me, ye that work iniquity."[22]

God does indeed give people the freedom to believe or disbelieve in him, unlike your claim that people are not permitted to believe as they wish. However, he clearly instructs his creation of the perils associated with separation from him: bondage to sin and eventual damnation are the final results of a godless lifestyle. If one makes a conscious decision to reject God's invitation to have a father-to-son relationship, then that person cannot aspire to be in the Lord's Kingdom. Be assured that anyone—regardless of the position society may ascribe to him—who claims to be a prophet after Jesus Christ is a charlatan in need of salvation. In addition, the Word of God is not measured in terms of numbers. At the time of the twelve apostles, the numbers of believers were in the hundreds, yet the zeal of the believers and the knowledge of the gospel was far more widespread. How does one identify a wolf in sheep's clothing? The Bible plainly indicates that they shall be known by their fruits[23], and their teachings should be judged in light of the Word of God. If a person then teaches that which is not in line with the Bible, and their actions (life) are not in line with the Scriptures, that person is a wolf in sheep's clothing.

There is no middle ground in the kingdom of God. One's soul is either saved or unsaved. There is no more chance to make things right in the grave

22. Matthew 7: 15–16; 21–23 (KJV).

23. See Matthew 7: 16.

and no such thing as half salvation. Preachers who preach a false sense of assurance besides the one clearly stated throughout Scripture (that is, salvation through confession of sins and acceptance of Jesus Christ as the only Savior) to their gullible and disillusioned followers shall face greater condemnation. The blame, however, falls upon lazy Christians as well, because they are commanded to read (search) the Scriptures, and stand by it, lest they be deceived.

Last, Christianity is not a religion of traditions, and there is no particular denomination that has the proper traditions but the Bible which is authoritative and serves as a point of reference for all believers. Christianity is faith in line with the Word of God; there is no way around it.

Dear friend, as always, your letters are highly appreciated, although we are at discord with each other on these deep and highly important questions.

Greetings and benedictions.

Yours truly,
Melchizedek

~

Wednesday, February 7, 1996
1939 Bemba Road
Kamda, Earthly Domain

Melchizedek,

One of the most ludicrous arguments consistently advanced by theists such as yourself is the notion that the words of your imaginary prophet, which were reportedly uttered some 2,000 years ago, are still relevant today. In fact, some Christians go as far as claiming that the teachings of Jesus Christ are more profitable today than when he taught them to his disciples. I haven't heard a greater lie than this one because it defies the laws of logic. How can words spoken thousands of years ago resonate more with reality today than in their own time? Christianity is synonymous with blind faith; therefore, I am not interested. It is also perplexing that your God created man with free will, but the end result is suffering, death, and eternal damnation. Your God is unloving for sending people to hell. If free will truly is something that is endowed by a Creator, there should be no punishment for its abuse. In my opinion, everyone should live according to their own desires and at the end of their lives, they should be welcome to an eternal life, if there is such a thing. In essence, I am advocating for a free ticket to heaven. It must be open, transparent, and welcoming to people of all gender, race, sexual orientation, and national origin. It mustn't be a club of preselected members who enjoy themselves while others suffer in a burning flame. Without compulsion from your God, everyone would live according to their own accord and there would be no fear of damnation after death.

It's outrageous that the opinions of certain religious leaders mean nothing to you. You have the audacity to belittle their positions to no significance and compare them to ordinary men? Dear friend, why? You, the religious friend, should not show such contempt to the positions of other religious men. It is true that no one is infallible, but you are too arrogant to assert that religious leaders are servants of Satan when they teach things contrary to the Word of your God.

If it is true that there are wolves in sheep clothing in churches then, there is a formidable dilemma that Christians face: Given the myriad of denominations that exist within Christianity, how can one know the right doctrine? What are the hallmarks of heretics? I can foresee you attempting to solve this dilemma by saying that the ultimate judgment rests with the supreme figure of your cult but this would be a pathetic answer that does not merit consideration let alone an answer. Also, what is the problem with the conception of a middleground that certain people hold dearly to their heart? Everyone deserves a second chance because we humans are prone to commit mistakes, and forgiveness is quintessential in moving forward. It is simply inconceivable then, to imagine a benevolent God who would be opposed to having a midway destination wherein sinful souls will be cleansed to enter his domain. In fact, dear Melchizedek you owe the followers of the so-called heretic teachings an apology, for unlike you, they try their best to give Christianity some semblance of worthiness.

Your friend,
Marawi

An Atheist's Letters to Heaven

Sunday, February 18, 1996
1517 Year Zero BCE Road
Paradise, God's Kingdom

Dear Brother,

The fact that you reject everything that has to do with Christianity but somehow speak out on what you view as its flaws baffles me. Never have I heard you point out positive aspects of Christianity. You are indeed a cynic, not a skeptic, because in spite of all the irrefutable proofs that I offered in defense of Christianity, it is as if you are a programmed machine that only allows and accepts things that are aligned with its existing data. So far, you have not offered any compelling alternative to God and heaven.

How ironic that you call God unloving since in your estimation he sends lost souls to hell. One fundamental blunder is to think God created hell for humans. I wrestled with this question when I was not part of the kingdom of God. In fact, within three days of my being welcomed to heaven, I posed the very question to the Lord. I, however, realized that God loves his children with an incomprehensive affection and has never intended harm for them. Hell is a result of the rebellion of Lucifer with his cohort of demons (fallen angels) who attempted to take over the Lord's throne. Alas, humans reject the constant invitation to be with God and choose to be with Satan in a place prepared for him and his demons for eternity. God has in eternity past known that man would fall into sin, therefore, instead of leaving man to his depravation, he offered his Son Jesus Christ as a substitute— the choice is for each person to make (the ball is in their court). This my friend, sums up what hell is meant for, and shows that humans choose to go to hell—not the Creator. Remember, just like Lucifer who shall face eternal damnation in the last judgment, it is rebellion, arrogance, self-justification (telling God that one wants to be his own god and in charge) that brings eternal punishment—not an act of God.

Hell is indeed not what most humans visualize it to be, and your statement about heaven: "it must be open, transparent, and welcoming to people of all gender, race, sexual orientation, and national origin," further substantiates this misconception. First, what gives you or any other person the prerogative to have a say in how the standard for hell ought to be set? The flawed notion of democracy and equality that humans hold to is nothing compared to the transparency and equity of God. Although God designed heaven for his creatures, there is no free ticket. If God admitted

128

evildoers, and those who despised his Word and died without having their hearts transformed by Jesus Christ and the Holy Spirit, into heaven, heaven would no longer be heaven: it would be as corrupt as the domain you dwell in called Earth. Consider these few questions: How would heaven be heaven with an unrepentant Hitler, Mao Zedong, Stalin, and Pol Pot in it? If all sinners and sin are permitted in heaven, how would it be a holy place with a holy God? If humans set the standard for heaven, what is the point of reference? You also advocated for everyone to live their lives with no reverence to the Word of God and your position is what brings about death, misery, and damnation to hell to start with. Satan, Adam, Eve, and the people gathered to build the Tower of Babel wanted to live in their own accord. That is what brought sin, suffering, death, and eventual damnation to the soul. So, should God be the one blamed? As long as mankind has been in existence, the Lord has sent his prophets, who people such as yourself call irrelevant and charlatan, and their warnings fell and continue to fall on deaf ears. One thing is certain: God's Word and the message he gave to his prophets in time past is more relevant and true in this day and age than ever before.

Furthermore, you erroneously assumed that if God did not exist, everyone would live according to their own accord and there would be no fear of damnation after death. This cannot be any further from reality, for there were and are societies plighted by war, human sacrifice, cannibalism, and other kinds of despicable acts, without reverence to the singular Creator. With no God and the lack of fear of eternal damnation, let me reiterate that there is nothing, and no reason, for anyone to make a moral judgment. Adultery, murder, robbery, covetousness, and racism, among others will be deemed normal and morally acceptable, and there is no reason to argue otherwise. The Bible shows that every time the children of Israel and the communities around them despised God, there was a mass proliferation of sin on an unimaginable scale: Human sacrifice, homosexuality, murder, adultery, and sodomy, to name a few. Today's society and its abominations also attest to this fact.

Moreover,

> That which was from the beginning, which we have heard, which we have seen with our eyes, which we have looked upon, and our hands have handle, of the Word of life; (For the life was manifested, and we have seen it, and bear witness, and shew unto you that eternal life, which was with the Father, and was manifested unto us;) That which we have seen and heard declare we unto you, that ye also may have fellowship with us: and truly our fellowship is with

the Father, and with his Son Jesus Christ. And these things write
we unto you, that your joy may be full. This then is the message
which we have heard of him, and declare unto you, that God is
light, and in him is no darkness at all.[24]

As this passage indicates, being a Christian is not synonymous with
blind faith. In fact, Christianity encourages its adherents to seek to know
God in an intimate manner. Nominal Christians have no knowledge of the
beauty and magnificence of the Creator. In this passage, it is evident that
John is saying that before time and the concept of logic, there existed a
self-evident entity that has been not only seen and heard, but the hands
of humans have handled (touched) him. Clearly, John is speaking about
Jesus Christ (the manifested image of God),with whom John walked, as his
contemporary, and saw him perform awesome miracles that bear witness to
the awesome and irrefutable omnipotence of God. As an eyewitness, John's
testament is highly reliable since it is a primary account. Furthermore, if
you talk to any true disciple—not the nominal Christians but those who
come to know the Father in an intimate manner—they will attest that belief in God is not driven but blind faith, but real-life personal experience,
whether in the form of miracles, supernatural experience, freedom from
depression and other personal struggles, or an inexplicable source of joy
and fellowship.

As a rebuttal to my assertion that those who claim to be followers of
Jesus Christ and teach doctrines contrary to the Word of the Father—also
known as wolves in sheep's clothing, you argue that if this is true, Christianity faces a dilemma. I am going to address your objections one at a
time. Christianity is not defined by the so-called myriad of denominations.
Be mindful that *denomination* is a man-made term that typically results
from a disagreement that believers have with fellow believers. In a bid to
set themselves apart and establish their own system of belief, they invent a
denomination that becomes their new identity. I strongly encourage you to
read the epistles of Paul to the first believers in Jerusalem and Asia Minor.
His letters yield a great deal of insight into the nature of man, even when
he claims to be at the service of God. There is nothing or any authority
that trumps the Bible. Although many characteristics distinguish a heretic,
there is none more obvious and truer than what Jesus spoke of, that they
should be known by their fruit.[25] The fact of the matter is that although a

24. 1 John 1:1–5 (KJV).
25. See Matthew 7:16–20.

person can deceive by his lips, and put on a superficial persona, the fruit of the work that the person leaves is a good indication of what he or she stands for. Jesus says that a "bad tree cannot produce good fruit, nor a goodly tree bad fruits."[26] Actions speak louder than words, and an end of a thing is more meaningful than the beginning thereof.[27]

It is a monumental blunder to assume that Christianity needs the approval of men to give it merit and worth. A middle place between earth and heaven to cleanse souls does not exist, and I am not going to retract this position because though it might be unpleasant, truth is always, and must be, the only option. You used human analogy and reason and inferred that everyone needs a second chance; hence, a middle ground ought to be an integral part of Christianity. Well, dear friend, what if I tell you that God has not only given humans a second chance but thousands of chances over the course of their lives? If you examine your life, for example, you will conclude that God has not only given you multiple chances—through conscience, encounters with evangelists, and so forth—and even now he allows you to communicate with a long-deceased friend. You, however, remain stiff-necked and defiant. You should read the story of the rich man who lived lavishly, died lost, and ended up in eternal damnation. Once in hell, he realized that the torment was unbearable. He, therefore, pleaded with Abraham to send the poor beggar (Lazarus) he neglected to dip the tip of his finger in water to cool his tongue. Realizing that this not possible, he request that Lazarus be sent to warn his brethren of the realities of hellfire. Abraham's answer was straight to the point: "They have Moses and the prophets; let them hear them. If they hear not Moses and the prophets, neither will they be persuaded, though one rose from the dead."[28]Indeed, God has revealed himself to humanity over the years and has made it clear how to attain eternal life. If humans then choose otherwise, that is their choice, and as the author of freewill, their wishes shall be honored. You also take the existence and severity of hell lightly because you do not realize God's holiness, perfection, and justice; in fact, he is the embodiment of these virtues, and cannot tolerate the slightest deviation from these virtues apart from the blood of Jesus Christ, for he had expelled Lucifer from heaven (one of his former angels, now known as Satan) because of pride

---

26. Matthew 7:18 (paraphrased).

27. See Ecclesiastes 7:8.

28. See Luke 16:19–31.

and impurity. Be assured that the concept of a middle ground between the earth and heaven is unscriptural and is not of God.

Like other atheists, you are playing with eternity because you fully put your faith and trust in the present life you have. One thing is certain, however: One can be alive physically but dead spiritually—sin kills a person, though he is still living.

Brother, do not play with eternity: it is too long to neglect.

Your friend,
Melchizedek

13

Witches, Warlocks, and Cults

Monday, March 18, 1996
1939 Bemba Road
Kamda, Earthly Domain

Dear Melchizedek,

You indeed went ballistic in your last letter and did not hide your true color: a hater of those who hold conflicting views and a promoter of closed-mindedness. Moreover, I am greatly offended that you have the audacity to call me a cynic and say that I turn a blind eye to proofs. What evidence are you speaking of? I have so far received no convincing and sound argument regarding the existence of your God, and there is a continuous dearth of valid argument and credibility for Christianity.

I would, however, like to discuss something you mentioned in your previous letter: the veneration of other personalities in addition to what your Bible prescribes. What is wrong with believing in saints and holy ones? What is the proper remedy to stop believers from following those you regard as teachers of falsehood? Doesn't your Bible claim that there are angels, a special type of saints, who live with your God in heaven?

You also inferred that one can be alive physically but dead spiritually. How can one be alive but dead? How does sin kill a person, though he is still living? What an oxymoron! Being alive is not about surrendering one's life to Christ but rather having the breath of life that allows one to inhale

133

and exhale air. Your repeated and sustained attempt to put mankind down in order to bolster the ego of your God is apparent and never-ending.

Last, do you believe in the existence of witches, warlocks, and cults? Many people, including those in the West, believe that witches, covens, and occult activities are not merely fictional creativity but reality. I personally do not allow myself to be brainwashed by such an obvious fraud and superstition. It would be interesting to know your position and that of your God, given that you believe in an entity called the devil.

I look forward to more foolishness from you.

Njerabé, Marawi

Tuesday, April 30, 1996
1517 Year Zero BCE Road
Paradise, God's Kingdom

My dear friend,

T he receipt of your letter always puts a smile on my face, for I very much enjoy corresponding with you. I am unsurprised that you are offended that I called you a cynic—not a skeptic. I meant no harm but was simply stating that which is obvious.

Over the course of our correspondence—over three years to be exact—I have offered numerous tangible and philosophical examples that prove that the existence of God is undeniable and nonfictional. Further, I point out real-life, historic events such as the ancient kingdom of Israel and its deportation to Assyria and Babylon, events recorded by your so-called secular scholars, and the life, death, and resurrection of Jesus Christ that the academia you often quotes agrees with. But just like the hardheaded people of Sodom and Gomorrah, you refuse to recognize a self-evident truth. What perhaps surprised me the most is that you were indignant because I invoke the dilemma that if there is no God, the moral issues that you raise and life itself would be meaningless, let alone metaphysical things such as the concept of love. Your reaction further proves that atheists and agnostics have no answer to the deep questions of life, but use the Christian God as a scapegoat, blaming all the problems brought about by sin on God and ascribing positive things to science, man, technology, or mother nature.

This is the problem that I have been cautioning you about all along, knowing that it is a lot easier to look at something or someone who you despise and point out his defects and flaws, than to realize your own imperfections and flaws. As long as there is no reference point and nothing to lean on, atheism will always fail when the same standards used to judge God and Christianity are applied to evaluate it.

As for the proper and most effective means to stop believers from following the perpetrators of falsehood and heretic teachers, the answer is simple: Believers should read their Bibles and ask God to open their hearts so that they can grasp the full understanding thereof. The problem is that most contemporary Christians are idle, for instead of reading the Word of God, they prefer to listen to prosperity teachers and men who teach out of their ego rather than the Word of God. I was having supper with the Lord last night and made mention of your inquiry regarding the subject at hand. At the end of the hall where we dine, there is a painting by Njerané Joab showing a Bible on a table. On the Bible is placed a hammer, then a cell phone, car keys, a soccer ball, and money on top. God's children have time for Facebook, vacation, cell phone, sports, and YouTube but claim to not have time to meditate on God's Word—no, not even for half an hour a day. This is how God's children's disdain of his Word, for they prioritize all these things (money, possessions, sports, job) above God. When believers do not exercise faith by reading the Word of God, they are naturally susceptible to the lies of charlatans. As the Lord said that my people are destroyed for lack of knowledge,[1] it is only through thorough knowledge and unwavering confidence in the Word of God that believers can put the lies of heretics to rest.

To answer your question regarding the title of sainthood that is given to some, don't forget that the Bible states that there is none righteous.[2] No. Not even one. Given that this is the position of the Bible—and naturally that of God, it is safe to conclude that there is no person worthy of the title Saint, unless used to refer to those who are saved, therefore made righteous before God through the cleansing blood of the Lamb. Angels, on the other hand, are different beings, for they are made higher than humans,[3] are immortal, and operate in a totally different realm. I do value virtuous individuals that accomplish noble deeds, such as the alleviation of poverty, the resolution of conflicts, living an upright and seemingly blameless life

---

1. See Hosea 4: 6.

2. Romans 3: 10.

3. See Hebrews 2: 6–8; Psalms 8: 4–5.

that inspires others to live likewise. However, dear friend, bear in mind that God looks at the heart more than deeds, for no thoughts or intentions can be hidden from him.[4] In this sense, no one is holy because although some may live an impeccable life, there is always a time that they have evil thoughts lurking in their mind and do unvirtuous deeds out of the sight of men, but not out of sight of God, from whom nothing can be hidden.

In Christianity, the word *saint* is only used to refer to saved believers who are justified by the blood of Christ—not to elevate or deify those who accomplish good works. Paul made this plainly clear: "As it is written, There is none righteous, no, not one."[5] Jesus' ministry shows that all humans are desperately lost in their sin and though they are living physically, they are dead in spirit. The only thing that sets people apart in the eyes of God is: those who have the courage and humility to let go of their sinful nature, confess their need for salvation, and opt to commune with God, and those who declare, "glory to man in the highest," are saying "I have no maker to whom I am accountable, and I can live my life as I see it fit without the fear of the final judgment" are thus condemned.

As for the question concerning what it means to be alive, remember that Jesus Christ said that he came to make dead people (those living in sin) live(set them free from sin).[6] This is not the physical life that you are speaking of (breathing air). It is much deeper than that. James said: what is the life of a man but a dew that appears for a moment and disappears.[7] Physical life is extremely limited in duration, and a person that does not have God in his life, though he lives, is dead. Sin keeps man in a perpetual state of servitude that equates to death, and Jesus Christ is the only One who can set souls free (make them alive). In contrast to your belief, Christianity does not seek to put man in a permanent state of dependency and servitude to God. In fact, the contrary is true: Christianity seeks to liberate man from sin and the deceptions of the world, to let him discover his true identity, that is, that he is made in the image of God and is meant to experience the wonders of his awesomeness.

Finally, as for the enemy, there is no such thing as fiction when it comes to the devil. The devil, with his agents, witches, warlocks, vampires, and cults, are real and do exist. This is assuredly a fact, not a fiction. Paul

4. See I Samuel 16: 7.

5. Romans 3: 10.

6. See John 10: 10.

7. See James 4: 14.

warned believers to put on the armor of God, for they wrestle not against flesh and blood, but against principalities, against powers, against the rulers of darkness of this world, against spiritual wickedness in high places.[8] The Bible mentions Satan and his agents (demons, witches, warlocks) on several occasions, including: "And the soul that turneth after such as have familiar spirits, and after wizards, to go a whoring after them, I will even set my face against that soul, and will cut him off from among his people."[9] It is becoming all the more common for the devil to blatantly show himself and gain more victims because so-called believers are growing increasingly unvigilant and insensitive to his devices. They do not read their Bible, but they allow Hollywood and other music and movie industries to repaint Satan as fiction.

There is a good book I read while living in the flesh called *The Art of War* by Sun Tzu. Although this is a book written from a secular, militaristic point of view, the author states, "If you know the enemy and know yourself, you need not fear the result of a hundred battles. If you know yourself but not the enemy, for every victory gained you will also suffer a defeat. If you know neither the enemy nor yourself, you will succumb in every battle."[10] This sums up the fate of unbelievers and negligent believers, who see satanic entities as fiction—they can learn from the principles outlined by Tzu, for Satan's best strategy is to make people believe that he is not real. The Christian life is a battle, not a vacation. As of the writing of this letter, dear friend, be assured that the enemy is taking over the world and is showing himself in the media, books, the internet, and other entertainment platforms. Furthermore, there are numerous examples of occult and satanic worship in the Bible, including Baal worship in the Levant, the abominable practices of the societies that preceded the children of Israel in the land of Canaan, and the fact that King Saul, the first king of Israel went to see a sorceress to raise the spirit of one of the prophets (Samuel) from the dead.[11] In fact, it is because of Satan's ability to take multiple forms and convince people that he does not exist that Christians are commanded to be extremely vigilant and exert optimal alertness, for Peter said, "Be sober, be vigilant; because your adversary the devil, as a roaring lion, walketh about, seeking whom he may devour: Whom resist stedfast in the faith, knowing

8. See Ephesians 6:10–12.

9. Leviticus 20:6 (KJV).

10. Sun Tzu, *The Art of War*, (London: Luzac & Company., 1910), 24–25.

11. See I Samuel 28

that the same afflictions are accomplished in your brethren that are in the world."[12] Warlocks, witches, sorcerers, magicians, cults, and their likes all operate as part of Satan's kingdom. They are neither myth, nor fantasy. For lack of doctrinal knowledge, Satan wants God's creatures to assume that he is not real, for if they are conscious of his existence, they would be less likely to become entrapped in the perpetual state of servitude to sin that leads to eternal damnation.

Any Christian who denies the existence of warlocks, sorcerers and cults is fooling himself, for there are several examples in the Scriptures that show that demonic entities are real: Jesus Christ chased demons out of many of his contemporaries; Paul blinded an irritating magician, and the battles between the Lord and his angels and Satan and his demons in the Book of Revelation. Although all humans are sinners, some become direct agents of Satan for diverse reasons, most notably, generational covenant made with a cult/coven; an uncontrollable quest and thirst for fame, riches, and power; participation in ungodly rituals forbidden by God such as the consultation of seers, psychics, yoga, astrology, ouija board; and entice-ment by peers who are already part of a satanic cult. Apostle Paul wrote at great length in one of his epistles that we wrestle not against flesh but against principalities,[13] implying that there is more to life than the physical world—a reality atheism and naturalism deny. Good and evil, virtue and vice, are locked in a constant battle before the last day when the forces of good (God's Kingdom) will emerge victorious over the forces of evil (Sa-tan's kingdom), thus putting an end to the status quo.

Let he who hath wisdom and knowledge heareth, and take heed thereto.

May the Lord of peace and understanding grant thee serenity and discernment.

Your Brother, Melchizedek

12. I Peter 5: 8–9 (KJV).
13. See Ephesians 6:12 (KJV).

14

Marawi's Incurable Maladies and God's Promise of Divine Healing

Friday, May 24, 1996
1939 Bemba Road
Kamda, Earthly Domain

Dear Brother,

I would like to apologize for the harsh words in my last letter. I am immensely grateful for having such an awesome friend whom I can communicate with even after death. What an unfeigned friendship and affection built on verity! Our brotherly love is genuine and neither death nor paradigmal difference can put an end to this candid relationship. It is, however, with an extremely saddened and broken heart that I must tell you that my life has abruptly changed for the worse, as I too shall soon leave the land of the living and join you in the afterlife.

Aside from the regular annual check-up and the occasional malaise that I consult my doctor for, he never unexpectedly asks me to come see him. Last Saturday around midday when I was at work, however, my doctor summoned me to his office. Although he refused to discuss the reason for the summon over the phone, I knew that something out of the ordinary must have come up in the last check-up results that I went for three days prior. At his insistence, I left work early and drove thirty minutes to go see him at Kaiser Permanente. I arrived and as I entered his office, I noticed the sinister environment: he was unusually quiet and avoided eye contact with me, as though my own doctor who has been taking care of me for decades was disturbed by my presence. After an extensive moment of silence, he motioned for me to sit down. He then took a deep sigh: "Mr. Marawi, I thank you for trusting me with your health all these years. It's been indeed a pleasure being your personal physician but unfortunately there are two sides to this job: the good and the bad, hope and hopelessness, happiness and sadness, life and death. As your physician, it is my duty to discuss your health with you, regardless of its nature. Having said that, the test results came in, and it is with deep regret that I must inform you that you have been diagnosed with stage four cancer, as well as AIDS—the most advanced stage of the HIV infection. I consulted my colleagues about your case, but they have all concluded that you only have three months to live. I am sincerely sorry."

Shock by this life-altering news, I put my head down and sobbed unceasingly. I refused to be consoled by the doctor, and upon my arrival home, I told my wife and three sons—Ithamar, Eleazar, and Cyrus—everything. The atmosphere at my house resembled that of a funeral home, as I wept on the shoulder of my wife. My three children shrieked, not knowing what to say or do. It was at that moment that I observed the fear of losing a husband in my wife's eyes and the fear of losing a father in my children's eyes. I laid there helpless, and the only thing that I could think of was my imminent death and the fact that my wife will become a widow and my children, orphans.

As if that was not enough, my wife informed me the next day that after consideration, she has decided to pursue the path of separation, and that she intends to acquire the house and the children, and that nothing would change her mind. Out of desperation, with no one and nothing to turn to, I informed my superior of the struggle I was going through. His answer caught me off guard: Mr. Marawi, unfortunately, there is nothing I can do for you. It is up to you if you want to keep working with us. You are no longer a productive asset to our company, and with your current health issues, you will be a liability and burden to our company—a burden this business cannot afford to have. My wife followed through with her vow and the following week, she left me, I quit my job, and am afflicted with two incurable diseases. My life has taken a U-turn and there is no reason for me to live anymore. It would be better had I not been born. I am presently an uninsured homeless man. I am persona non grata to my own wife and children.

Brother Marawi, how can I endure these trials? I have spent all of my life having faith in myself and thinking that there is nothing that can bring me down. Indeed, I believed for many years that I am unbeatable and there is no disease or problem that I am not immune to. Alas, at this moment, life has shown me its true color. I mourn everything and everyone I lost. How do Christian deal with pain and suffering? Thinking that I am a god, and that man is nothing but a combination of particles does not cure my plights. Suffering and pain are real, and unfortunately, the atheism that I fought for so hard over the years offers no consolation, let alone a solution. At this point, I have lost everything that I hold dearly to my heart: My wife and children, my health and ability to do the things I used to do, my job, house, and Mercedes. I am, in essence, a walking dead man.

Dear friend, I am aware that my days are numbered. Be assured of one thing before I leave the land of the living: You are truly a brother of mine, for you were and are always there for me in times of joy and sorrow.

You have dedicated a great deal of time, trying to convince me to subscribe to your Christianity but I have chosen to die as an atheist, regardless of the potential cost.

Farewell brother.
Your soon-to-be deceased brother Njerabé

Sunday, June 9, 1996
1517 Year Zero BCE Road
Paradise, God's Kingdom

Greetings my esteemed friend,

I am writing to express my most sincere sympathy and compassion to you, for it is not God's plan that his creatures shall suffer—it is that of the prince of your domain called the devil. Abide in the Word of God which says: "Ask, and it shall be given you; seek, and ye shall find; knock, and it shall be opened unto you: For every one that asketh receiveth; and he that seeketh findeth; and to him that knocketh it shall be opened."[1] First and foremost, be assured that God has given his children the spirit of bravery—not of fear. In this tragic moment, you ought to accept Christ in order to

1. Matthew 7: 7–8 (KJV).

become a child of the Lord. God is love and there is no fear in perfect love, for perfect love cast away fear.

Upon reading your letter, I pleaded your case before the Lord and his Son during the evening supper. In response, he reassured me not to panic or suffer my soul for you. God, the omnipotent and omniscient— Adonai and Jehovah-Rapha (my healer) loves you dearly. You shall not die brother, nor will a hair fall from your head, for the Lord's time is not at hand. He is going to turn this tragedy brought upon you by Satan to snatch you out of his hand and send your soul to eternal damnation into an awesome deliverance that shall cast away all the lies and doubts that the enemy has placed in your heart. God will transform your heart so that you can come to know your heavenly Father. Remember the story of Joseph (who is currently with us in Paradise) who was sold by his brethren to an Ishmaelite caravan? Although this was done to his detriment, God overturned the work of the wicked and exalted him to the rank of second-in-command in Egypt, as Joseph himself exclaimed: "Now therefore be not grieved, nor angry with yourselves, that ye sold me hither: for God did send me before you to preserve life."[2]

Though still an unbeliever, I strongly encourage you to read the story of Job, and realize that the safest place to be in a storm for a child of God is the eye of the storm. God can be your shelter in a time of storm but you must repent before it is eternally too late. Be mindful that though you are inundated by negative thoughts and overcome by fear, you can welcome Christ into your heart and find solace in the God of your salvation; as a believer, you will keep fighting the good fight of faith. A believer diagnosed with a terminal illness has the assurance that God will not forsake him, and even if it comes down to the death of the temporal temple called body, he has the assurance that his soul shall abide eternally with the Creator in his heavenly domain. A godless person, however, has nowhere and nothing to turn to, and believes that there is no hope beyond the grave: he tries to hold onto the present life and is terrified by the idea of death. These two elements sometimes end up precipitating an unbeliever's death as he loses hope and his physical body becomes overstressed. The spirit then naturally follows.

As for your doctor and his so-called colleagues, they are human and prone to use fallible logic to draw conclusions. They concluded that you have only three more months left on Planet Earth based on man-made machines and trends that do not affect the way God operates, nor place a

2. Genesis 45: 5 (KJV).

limit on what he can do. Although God's understanding and power are well beyond that of humans, often the living think that whatever doctors decree, which is based on "expertise" that amounts to nothing but foolishness in the eyes of God—must be accurate and unchallenged. This is the same God in flesh that defied the laws of nature and physics by silencing the storm and walking on water. He is able to turn your ashes into beauty.

When it comes to terminal illnesses, two basic fundamentals determine the outcome and the longevity of the person enduring the infirmity: his attitude vis-à-vis the malady and his personal stance with God. Marawi, cancer, HIV, COVID-19, diabetes, and any of the other dreaded diseases are a result of sin and collectively constitute the effort of Satan to attack and destroy the physical body, for he knows that most humans' faith will waver and they will succumb to death if a name of a dreaded disease is associated with them. In fact, many individuals who depart the land of living due to diseases do so because they allow themselves to be mentally defeated, thereby their body naturally follows as it deteriorates and the enemy gets his way. You, on the other hand, I expect to endure this infirmity in faith, bravery, fortitude, and cede not even an inch to the devil.

One thing you must keep in mind while enduring this trial is the reality that personality and character is not built in time of happiness and when everything is going well. True character comes about in time of adversity and tremendous suffering. A distance runner does not become a part of the elite group overnight but through arduous, persistent training. Know that God is allowing your character to develop, and you will be a much stronger and a greater asset for him after this temporary moment of adversity and suffering subsides. How can a person who has never endured great sickness understand what sickness is in order to counsel another who is ill? How can someone who has never experienced destitution sympathize with the destitute? How can someone who has never experienced the love and joy of God talk to another about the love and joy of God? Do not lose heart and in due time, you will look back and thank God for allowing you to go through this trial; for the God of the mountain is still Lord in the valley.

I am sorry to hear that your wife and sons have parted from you. Humans often fail to define love and too often end up leaving the person they confess to love at the time he or she needs them the most. The Bible states that God is love and in him, there is no darkness.[3] Contrary to popular belief, love is neither a feeling nor an emotion. Love is personified in the

---

3. See I John 1: 5; I John 4: 7.

entity of God the Father and is an action verb rather than a noun. No one can give what he or she does not have. Because you and your wife did not have the love of God in you, the mere "I love you" that has been reciprocally uttered from the time of courtship to marriage has no root (foundation), as evidenced by your wife's action as soon as she learned that you contracted two terminal diseases and was given only three months to live. John 3:16 reads, "For God so loved the world, that he gave his only begotten Son, that whosoever believeth in him should not perish, but have everlasting life." Your wife may have a deep admiration for you but not love, for love is patient and goes above and beyond the confines of logic—it is sacrificial, not selfish.

Moreover, the loss of everything that you hold dear to your heart is precisely why the Word of says: "Lay not for yourselves treasures upon the earth, where moth and rust doth corrupt, and where thieves break through and steal: But lay up for yourselves treasures in heaven, where neither moth nor dust corrupt, and where thieves do not break through nor steal: For where your treasure is, there will your heart be also."[4] Most of the things people spend the majority of their lives working for are not worthy, for tragedy and death render them obsolete—"As he came forth of his mother's womb, naked shall he return to go as he came, and shall take nothing of his labor, which he may carry away in his hand,"[5] the Bible says.

Alas, it took the solitude of this tragic news for you to realize that atheism has no answer to the real and genuine suffering of humans. Nonetheless, it is profitable that you realized this sooner than later—repent, delay not.

How long, dear Marawi, shall you halt between two gods—the supreme and true one in heaven and the god of man in your domain. If God be God, worship him, if science is your god then remain stiff-necked and face the consequence of your stubbornness. Jesus Christ cautions believers against duplicity when he said: "No man can serve two masters: for either he will hate the one, and love the other; or else he will hold to the one, and despise the other. Ye cannot serve God and mammon." Be careful which master you choose to serve and place your faith in.[6]

Dear friend, I am moved with compassion because of the hardship you are enduring. Now, be more serious with the God who has been patiently waiting for you to come to him. Due to your continued unbelief, I

4. Matthew 7: 19–21.

5. Ecclesiastes 5: 15 (KJV).

6. Matthew 6: 24 (KJV).

advise that you do not set foot in hospital nor consult your doctor, for you will realize the awesome power of God, and forsake the misconception that he is a distant, fictional entity.

Be strong and positive.

Your brother Melchizedek

Sunday, July 21, 1996
1939 Bemba Road
Kamda, Earthly Domain

Dear Melchizedek,

Thank you for taking the time to read my letter and sympathize with me. I have literally no one to turn to in this difficult moment, and frankly if it weren't for you, I would have taken my life by now—the pain is just too immense to bear alone. Whether Satan has his hands in what is happening to me, I do not know. One thing is certain, however, the presence of a dark energy can be traced in this tragedy. I applaud you on showing an unwavering and firm faith in the God that you worship. I, however, remain unconvinced and will not put my faith in an unseen force. I do appreciate the steps that you have taken as a brother to help me, and I enjoyed reading the story of Job. The story is beneficial to any human being regardless of his or her belief because it offers many life lessons and solace in the moment of solitude. I shared your last letter and asked my friends whether they believe in healing by God. They laughed it to scorn, and we unanimously agreed that it is not possible that the energy of an unseen force is greater than the expertise of medical experts. Therefore, we have decided to put your words to the test: I will heed your instruction and not set foot in any hospital again. Instead, I will post my diagnosis as well as your last letter on Facebook, YouTube, Instagram, MySpace, and Twitter. There are only two possible results: (1) I die and everyone will realize that the Christian God is a charlatan and fiction, or (2) I miraculously recover my health, in which case the credit has to go to your God, and I will have no other choice but to become a believer. The fate of your God in our estimation—as well as the discussions that we have been having over the years for me to become a believer in Christ—rests on the outcome of my health, since you have always stated that your God is not a man that he should lie.

I heard of the struggle between the forces of evil and good wrestling within man in the invisible realm, but never thought that Christianity would confirm this. I remain unconvinced that Satan has his hands in every tragic event that happens in the lives of humans to sabotage the plans of your God. Christians tend to credit their God with everything positive that happens to them, while blaming anything bad that happens to them on Satan. In my case, *misfortune* is the more appropriate adjective because as far as I am concerned, there is no battle raging for my loyalty and/or destiny. I assume this is the reason why you mentioned that I should become a believer and keep "fighting the good fight of faith." I, frankly, have no idea what you are talking about, and am clueless about what the good fight of faith entails. If you can clarify this point in your next letter, it would be highly appreciated.

I am also shocked that you said that the expertise of those in the medical field is inherently flawed because they use man-made machines, trends, and their conclusions account for nothing but foolishness in the eyes of your God. It's discouraging to realize that after having these discussions for years, you are still unconvinced and unimpressed with the scientific method. Whether you like or not, trends, expertise, and patterns do not lie. If it is indeed true that your God can change the outcome of a person's medical situation, then why do Christians who pray to receive divine healing also die a miserable death at the hospital? As for what determines how long a person lives after diagnosis of a terminal illness, I do agree that a person's attitude is vital but not in the same sense as you. Your life is so consumed by the preoccupation of the imaginary deity that you cannot see things as they are: One's stance with God has nothing to do with longevity in sickness. Quite the contrary, the person who has no God, pursues a practical and proactive approach of consulting the experts in the medical field, thereby increasing his chance of acquiring a remedy or cure.

The mental battle greatly shapes the outcome of one's battle with a terminal illness. What I disagree with is the insertion of your God's name in the conversation and the blame put on Satan. It's a psychological reality that can be understood by simple logic and there is no reason to think otherwise. Further, you babbled and spoke rubbish when you stated that "this misfortune came upon me for my own good, for my character is being built, and I will be a much more effective asset to those who will go through similar trials later in life." How can anybody with sanity reason thus? No sane person knowingly commits an accident and hopes to be a better and more cautious driver after survival. Your statement simply defies logic, and I am in no mood to be entertained by such foolishness. Perhaps, you underestimate the extent of the physical, financial, and emotional calamity that I endure. It is this very mindset that immobilizes Christians and keeps them dependent instead of solving their issues. They blame Satan and remain idle, hoping to be rewarded by their imaginary God someday. I refuse to let myself fall into a permanent state of victimhood and have vain hope.

What gave you the impression that I'm interested in being lectured on the meaning of love? Although you and I have known each other for a while, you have not the slightest idea about my wife, nor have a clue about the condition of our marital relationship before I was diagnosed with stage four cancer. Saying that your God is the embodiment of love undermines the most important aspect of love—that is the pleasurable real experience that those who are in love enjoy. Emotions and feelings do define love because anyone who is in love will develop feelings for the other person and become emotionally attached. I am frankly offended by the lack of respect for my marital life and the advancement of a claim that is groundless and moronic. Please keep such nonsensical statements to yourself. I am focused on nothing but recovering my health at the moment.

Last, brother, do not assume that just because I came to realize that atheism offers nothing at a time of solitude, that I converted to your cult. I need much, much more irrefutable and convincing evidence before I can even consider forgoing my atheistic beliefs.

Behold, my time to depart the material and physical life is at hand, per my doctor. I know not what shall happen after this letter. I, however, made the experiment public on all my social media accounts. Now it's up to the public to judge whether your God is genuine or not. If I die, he is a liar; but if I miraculously recover my health, thereby defying the words of qualified physicians, he is genuine and deserves our loyalty.

Adieu Brother Melchizedek.
Njerabé, Marawi

Thursday, November 21, 1996
1517 Year Zero BCE Road
Paradise, God's Kingdom

Beloved Marawi,

I have knowingly delayed my response to your latest letter, for you continue to display a great deal of pride and lack of faith. I am writing in
the surety of you being alive and well despite the prediction of the medical experts. You continue to take the promise of God as fiction and mere
babbling. The Bible says that God cannot and should not be tested. He is
neither limited by social media platforms, nor friends therein. Jesus Christ
said, "It is written again, Thou shalt not tempt the Lord thy God."[7] It is unwise to submit divine promise to the experimentation of mortal scientists.
You are supposed to be dead over three months ago according to the words
of the doctors. So far, God has made good on his promise that not a hair
will fall from your head, nor is it your time to depart the land of the living.

I, however, found it extremely refreshing that you enjoyed reading the
story of Job even as an atheist and secularist. The truth of the matter is that
the Word of God is so powerful that even a nonbeliever can benefit from
reading it, for wisdom, life, and knowledge are therein. Inform your peers
and those who doubt Almighty God to be ready for the fulfillment of his
promises in your life. In fact, in exactly one month from the writing of this
letter, everything that you lost shall be restored to you within a span of three
days: On December 21st, go consult your doctor to confirm that the cancer
and the AIDS virus have fully left your body; on the 22nd of December, be
ready to be reunited with your wife and children, and on December 23rd,
God will take care of your desire to regain your lost employment, although
he has a far better plan for you. Please bear in mind that God's plan for your
life is greater than a mere job and in due time, you will realize who you are
meant to work for and serve on earth.

As for the things that you enquired of in your last letter, there is indeed a raging battle in the spiritual realm between the forces of good/virtue
(God) and the forces of evil/vice (Satan) for the soul of every person. This
is no fiction and every decision that a human makes has tremendous repercussions on his soul in the spiritual realm. The forces of good manifest
themselves in every human life in the form of conscience and benevolent,

7. Matthew 4: 7 (KJV).

148

godly advice from others: It's the voice that quietly tells one not to act or make a decision that one knows is wrong and an offense to God; the co-worker, kinsman, or friend who God uses to dissuade one from going down a wrong path and encourages one to accept Christ. The forces of evil, on the other hand, manifest themselves in the form of destructive temptations, bad advice from those close to one, ignorance of one's need for the cleansing blood of Christ (salvation), and decisions taken without praying to God and having peace beforehand.

You accuse Christians of attributing anything positive to God while blaming the devil for everything bad that happens to them. Well, have you considered atheists and unbelievers who blame the Christian God for everything bad that has occurred and currently taking place in your domain—diseases, wars, deaths, poverty—while crediting science and mankind for every good thing that happens? God is a just God and there is no ill intention in him. He has a good plan for each and every human being. It's humans who chose otherwise and suffer as a result of rebellion and their choice to partake with Satan in his evil deeds and devices.

Fighting the good fight of faith means that in spite of believer's decision to defy the commands of God, thereby falling in the snare of Satan, and consequently suffering tremendously; one must remember that the love and mercy of God have not been rescinded: It's enduring suffering and the unknown with faith and assurance that God is in control regardless of one's past mistakes and the odds. You also offered a sharp criticism to the point I made regarding the problems associated with being fully reliant on the words of those in the medical field. In your criticism, you stress that despite the extent and scope of our discussions, it's discouraging that I undervalue the scientific method. Beloved, do not be so hardheaded and stiff-necked, for the personhood of God constitutes the beginning of knowledge, and he is the one who gave those doctors, in whom you are so confident, the breath of life and the knowledge to heal the body of patients.

In responding to your question regarding why some Christians end up yielding the ghost despite the fact that they have extensively prayed for the healing of their body, it is important to consider the reverse of the question: Why can't the scientific method and physicians heal every sick individual? The truth of the matter is that though a believer fights the fight of faith and prays to God for deliverance from suffering, the ultimate decision rests with God, and humans cannot fully comprehend the things of God, nor his ways. He, at times, delays his answer to strengthen the bond between that individual and himself; God, sometimes, calls the believer home to be with him; but in certain situations, he grants instantaneous miraculous healing. The fact of the matter is that God has the best intention in mind for each and all of his children and rescues them in the time of hardship in diverse manners. One thing is certain, however: when someone walks with God, there is hope—a hope that surpasses temporal life on earth and the worst suffering the enemy can throw in a believer's direction. One the other hand, when one does not have God in his life and fully relies on physicians to heal him, his hope is vain because he can depart the land of the living at any moment that the giver of life takes the breath from him, and after that he shall appear unprepared before God Almighty for the last judgment.

I cannot help but include God in all my views on every single issue. He defines my paradigm because his Spirit lives in me. It's however, untrue that one's relationship with God has nothing to do with one's longevity after diagnosis with a terminal illness. The secular scientists that you continue to quote agree with this fact as well and numerous studies conducted by secular researchers confirm that believers in God typically have a greater peace of mind and on average live longer when confronted with incurable disease than unbelievers. A faith in God helps an individual cope with terminal illness and live longer in two fundamental ways. First, when the victim is a believer, he casts his stress and worries on God, as he abides in the assurance of the following words spoken by Jesus Christ: "Come unto me, all ye that labour and are heavy laden, and I will give you rest."[8] Stress is notorious for being one of the leading causes of death in patients with terminal illness because when the mind is defeated, the body follows.

It has never been my intention to belittle the degree of the physical, financial, and mental hardship you are going through, nor do I intend to bring you down. I was simply stating the obvious that although it is undesirable for any human to suffer, it's through suffering that a true and lasting character is built. A wise man once said that a faith that cannot be tested cannot be trusted. In my case, I would have neither become the strong Christian that I was, nor attained eternal life, had I not lost my parents on that shipwreck during their voyage from Lebanon to Chad. It is indeed for this reason that the Bible says that "And we know that all things work together for good to them that love God, to them who are the called according to his purpose."[9]

8. Matthew 11: 28 (KJV).
9. Romans 8: 28 (KJV).

I also did not mean to attack your marital relationship but rather to define the true meaning of love so that the sentimental heartache that you are enduring can be averted next time. Contrary to your persistence that love is defined by emotions and feeling, God is the embodiment of love, and anybody who does not have the Lord neither has love, nor can give it. When fire is lit, there is smoke. Although there is smoke, the smoke does not explain itself or its source: the source and inciter is fire. Likewise, emotions, feeling, and pleasure do not define love—God does. I need not have a profound knowledge about your marital life to conclude that it was troublesome and lacks a strong foundation, for the Bible teaches that marriage and love constitute a lifelong commitment, with both partners willing to go through the highs and lows of life together, not forsaking the other in a time of trouble and hardship. The fact that your wife left you as soon as she learned of your diagnosis further confirms the reality of the lack of the biblical definition of marriage in your home.

Last, I am not concerned about your current view on God because I am convinced that the Holy Spirit will finish the work he started and will make you a new creature.

I look forward to receiving the news of your healing and that of the restitution of everything you lost in the next letter.

Best regards,
Your Brother Melchizedek

15

Marawi's Recovery and the
Restoration of Everything he Lost

Wednesday, January 1, 1997
1939 Bemba Road
Kamda, Earthly Domain

Happy New Year!

May the prosperity and blessings of your Lord come upon you this year. I am exceeding happy to have received your response. Most importantly, I am writing to inform you that all the promises that your God made to me came to pass. Indeed, it's not only I who am in awe of the wondrous miracles performed by the deity you worship but my whole entourage and those who shared the experiment on social media.

As soon as I finished reading your last letter, I started to feel better and the symptoms of my maladies started to fade. At first, I thought it was my thoughts but as the days went by, I could not help but realize that my body was being healed. On December 21st—one month after the receipt of your letter, I went to a local clinic for a test to see whether cancer and HIV had left my body. To my surprise, the doctor confirmed that there was no sign of either disease in my body. I refused to believe and contacted my doctor who invited me to his office for follow-up exams. While I was waiting for the results of the exams—on the morrow—my wife called me out of the blue and told me that she would like to speak to me that selfsame day. I was bewildered but decided to go meet her at the Lacosta Restaurant in downtown Kamda. As soon as I entered the premise, I noticed a different countenance and demeanor on my wife: she seemed happy and welcoming—an appearance that I had not seen since my diagnosis. As we started to converse, she unexpectedly said: "Dear husband, I have been thinking a lot these last few months. It's extremely difficult to raise the kids by myself and I must confess I miss my Marawi. This last month, I don't know what it is, but I cannot pass a minute without thinking about you. I also keep hearing a calm voice inside me saying, 'go!—reconcile with your husband.' After an extensive time thinking, I have decided to come home with the children, and see what destiny has in store for us." I was shocked and at a loss for words, for I could not believe the miracle that was taking place right before my eyes.

Last, on the third day, my former employer who encouraged me to resign, deeming me worthless, phoned me and stated that since my departure, the company had unsuccessfully attempted to fill my position, and consequently was incurring a tremendous financial loss. He informed me that I was re-offered the job, with double salary, and a benefit package that includes healthcare coverage for the entire family and a Ferrari with a personal chauffeur. I did not know how to process the call and could not help but think about the things you said in your latest note.

At last, the results of the follow-up exams ordered by my doctor came in, but my doctor still did not believe the results and compelled me to undergo another round of tests. This time, he sent me to the Cleveland Clinic in Ohio, since it is one of the most trusted hospitals in the world, with cutting-edge technology. After obtaining my blood sample and other pertinent samples, the exam was completed. I was informed that the results would be forwarded directly to my personal doctor. Cleveland Clinic sent the results of the exams one week later, and they were all negative. Startled by the results, Doctor Abihud Njekilamian Zadok stated that during his nearly 45 years of practice, he has never witnessed such a thing. He went on to say that he mocks the Christian God and fully relies on science and his medical expertise, but henceforth he will reexamine his position and look into claims in the Bible.

As promised, at the conclusion of the miracles, I shared on social media all the things that my deceased friend and his God have spoken of and came to pass. People were skeptical at first, but as time went by and I posted the results of the tests performed by my doctor and the follow-up tests, they did not know how to make sense of it all with human logic. As I have pointed out numerous times before, I am a man who relies heavily on empirical and testable data to draw a conclusion. Having said that, given the convincing arguments that you have offered in regard to Christianity, and the miracles that your God has wrought in my life—though I despised and scorned him, I am now considering Christianity. A clear sign, however, has to be manifested before I would consider becoming a believer. This time, it cannot be a dream, for I am on the verge of making one of the hardest and most crucial decisions in my life.

Dear brother, I am more thankful now than ever that I've gotten to know you—not just in the physical and material world but now in the afterlife. You have been a great companion and an indispensable source of support to me during the arduous and trying times that I have just come through. Words cannot express the joy that I feel and the sense of added meaning to life I experience. The spiritual realm is real—atheism is indeed dead and lacks substance!

I charge you with my most sincere salutations and deepest gratitude to pass on to whoever may have contributed to my healing and the restoration of everything I lost. I look forward to receiving your response and am anxious to find clarity in the next step of my life.

Cheers!
Brother Marawi

Monday, February 3, 1997
1517 Year Zero BCE Road
Paradise, God's Kingdom

Dear Brother,

Thank you for updating me on the great news that God has brought everything he promised to pass. I am sure that you are now seeing that the God I serve is not like other gods created by man's hand that can neither talk nor hear. I rejoice the more that the seed has also been planted in Doctor Abihud's heart as he realizes that there is a power greater than science and expertise. I am certain that the bond between you, your wife and children will be stronger than ever, since you all overcame a tremendous challenge by the grace of the Lord.

I applaud your decision to consider Christianity as a possible way forward. You have indeed come a long way from where you were at the beginning of this correspondence when you did not want to hear about the God I worship or the Holy Book, the Bible. It is perfectly fine that you genuinely avail yourself to receive a clear revelation from the Lord about how to believe in him. I have spoken to your Creator about this and he informed me that three days from the receipt of this note, a certain evangelist named Absalom Rehoboam shall come knock at your door and inform you what to do next. Listen to everything that he tells you, for God is going to connect you with an appropriate congregation of believers to draw you to himself and instruct you with exactitude about the Word of God.

Dear Brother, wait until this man comes to you, and you shall yet see another miracle from the Lord.

Sincerely yours,
Your Brother, Melchizedek

16

Marawi's Conversion to Christianity and Elation in Heaven

Friday, March 07, 1997
1939 Bemba Road
Kamda, Earthly Domain

Greetings from the earth God created!

B lessed be my soul! I very much enjoyed reading your letter and am writing to inform you that I have at last made a profession of faith! I rejoice the more that I've finally come to discover the true source of joy, love, and purposeful living. Quite a bit has changed in my life since your last letter, and I am writing to inform you that the things that God has spoken concerning how I would find his clear revelation happened as he stated.

Three days after the receipt of your letter (on a Friday evening to be exact), a young man came and knocked at the door of my house. My wife went to open the door and asked the man who he was and what he wanted. He quietly replied, "My name is Absalom Rehoboam and I am sent by the Lord to come and see Brother Njerabé Marawi. I am the brother of your friend Bonodji Abishag." Startled and skeptical, my wife called and asked if I knew anyone with the name of Rehoboam, the brother of Bonodji. I immediately recognized the name and told her to invite him to enter. Upon entering, he kissed me on both cheeks and proceeded to ask me a series of questions regarding my stance with God and how I intend to get to know him more intimately. His questions were thought-provoking, and he told me things about my life that no one could know except an all-knowing God. Before leaving, brother Absalom Rehoboam said that I was invited to a certain church called EET N*18, led by Pastor Njéla Timothy, and that I was highly encouraged to bring my family and any other willing lost soul along with me.

On that Sunday, I invited my family, my doctor, and all my non-Christian friends to go and hear the preaching of the man of God. We arrived at EET N*18 at 11AM for the morning service. Upon our arrival, we noticed a totally different environment—unlike anything we have been used to before: the attendees were genuinely happy, the songs that gave praise to God were authentic, and the members sang with passion. Although it was our first time, we were immediately treated as members of the church family. I must confess that although I have been to several social gatherings such as parties, nightclubs, and educational institutions, none of them resemble what I saw and felt at the church that day. Upon collecting the offering and the acknowledgment of the guests present, the preacher commenced the preaching. The message he delivered that day was titled, "The Sin of Man and the Invitation of God for Redemption." his sermon, which was based on John 3:16, was memorable and powerful, and at the conclusion all of us present felt as if the preacher was speaking to each of us directly. Pastor Njéla talked about how sin entered the world, the lostness and rebellion of man, the coming and death of Jesus Christ (the blood of the Lamb), the diverse sin that man commit, the limited time that man has on Planet Earth, and the final judgment that all will face. He quoted Amos 4: 12 and told us why, how, and when we should prepare to make our Creator God.

At the end of the message, Pastor Timothy invited everyone who had not yet accepted Jesus Christ as their personal Lord and Savior to the altar. Although convicted, like Pilate who stared at the embodiment of truth and turned the other way, we all refused at first; we feared the judgment of men, should we become believers. However, as the preacher insisted that he sensed someone in the edifice wanted to give his life to Christ but feared man, and this may be the last time God extended his invitation to that person, the Holy Spirit started to draw me. He then glanced directly at me, and I could no longer feel any resistance in myself and got up, walked to the altar, and knelt down and started to weep unceasingly. To my surprise, my family, my doctor, and all the peers present followed me. We all wept bitterly and after the service when the Pastor asked us individually if we were ready to follow Jesus Christ, and become God's children, we all replied with a resounding yes! We were subsequently baptized and became members of

EET N*18 from that day, and we attend the Sunday service regularly. More-over, we have a Bible study session every Wednesday and share the passages we read in the Bible during the week. The goal is to complete reading the Bible by the end of the year.

Dearly beloved in the Lord, I am infinitely grateful to you for leading me to the pathway of salvation. I was indeed lost, negligent, and proud as an atheist. Now I realize the true meaning of "And ye shall know the truth, and the truth shall make you free."[1] Like the lost prodigal son, I am found by the Father.

Arise ye soldiers of the Cross, for the vilest sinner is found!
In Christ,

Brother Marawi Njerabé

Wednesday, April 09, 1997
1517 Year Zero BCE Road
Paradise, God's Kingdom

My Brother in the Lord,

I, my Father, Jesus Christ the Son, and the host of heavenly angels are rejoicing greatly because you have finally accepted the call of God to become his child. In response to your confession, Jesus Christ will honor what he said: "Whosoever therefore shall confess me before men, him will I confess also before my Father which is in heaven."[2] As customary, there is a celebration in heaven every time a lost soul is found. Brother Jephthah Abiathar is charged with organizing the celebration for your salvation. It's been a long, arduous endeavor to bring you to Christ, but all the effort is worth it because I am at peace, for my brother will join me where I am at the appointed time.

As for your new life as a believer in Christ, know that Christianity is a relationship and does not have a complicated method of conversion. It's a simple threefold step that consists of one's acknowledgment as sinner, accep-tance of Jesus Christ's death on Calvary, and confession that he is the only way to the Father (God). Following conversion is a lifelong journey to conform to

1. John 8: 32 (KJV).
2. Matthew 10:32 (KJV).

the image of Christ. "Therefore if any man be in Christ, he is a new creature: old things are passed away; behold, all things are become new."[3] Therefore, brother, as a believer in Christ, forsake all your old ways (sin), and set your eyes on the kingdom of God (strive to be more like Christ). For your spiritual growth, continue to read the Bible. Behold, God sent his servant Absalom Rehoboam to guide you in the next step(s). In three weeks, he will come and knock at your door again to confirm the calling of God upon your life. As a note of advice, be very vigilant; put on the armor of God, for there is a battle raging in the spiritual realm to lure you away from your newfound hope and faith. Be mindful not to repeat the same sinful acts that you were guilty of prior to your conversion. Always speak in love to edify your brethren—refrain from lying and slandering. Do not charge usury to your brother who lacks. Refrain from extramarital affairs and going to nightclubs and bars. Above all, acknowledge the sovereignty of Jesus Christ in all your decisions: he must be your all in all—not just an added accessory to your life. You are a highly intelligent young man, keen for godly knowledge; therefore, I trust that you will make time to spend time with God spiritually by reading the Bible from cover to cover and praying to the Almighty—prayer is your best ally and source of strength in your Christian walk. The Holy Spirit has been by your side since the day you expressed the desire to know this wonderful God and his Son Jesus Christ. He will be guiding you in your new spiritual walk and shall illuminate the Scriptures for you.

As a new believer, I suggest you pay special attention to a few books in the Bible and characters that were in a similar stage as yourself. The books that I suggest are Proverbs, Psalms, and the four Gospels—Matthew, Mark, Luke, and John. Please beware that all Scripture is inspired by God for profit of mankind, but there are different passages that resonate much more with individuals. You should read the Bible from cover to cover and pay special attention to the following individuals: David, Paul, Thomas, and Hezekiah. These biblical characters have characteristics that you can identify with and can acquire a great deal of knowledge from them.

In sum, I am enthralled that you finally humbled yourself and acknowledged the Creator and confessed the name of Jesus Christ as your Lord and Savior. I look forward to receiving your next letter, informing me on your spiritual progress and confirming God's plans for your life.

Cordially,
Your brother in Christ.

3. II Corinthians 5: 17 (KJV).

17

Marawi Surrenders to Become a Missionary

Sunday, May 4, 1997
1939 Bemba Road
Kamda, Earthly Domain

My dear brother in Christ!

I am writing to inform you that evangelist Absalom Rehoboam stopped by to speak with me as you predicted. We chatted for nearly three hours, and this time we talked more about my work and future plans for my life. Before he left, Bro. Rehoboam informed me that God has a special plan for my life and that I should pray and mention a certain place called Bandiaterra in my prayer. Not being entirely certain about the details of this providential instruction, I prayed as he instructed me.

The following day, I went to work but no longer had the desire to work there. It was as if my heart had been transformed. I also lost interest in the decent salary, the health insurance, and the fancy vehicle with the personal chauffeur. I started to have a grander and more profound vision for my future: to serve God full time and see where he leads me. I discussed my change of plans and passion with my wife at the evening super, and she, surprisingly, informed me that God had placed the same burden in her heart. She, therefore, suggested that we pray corporately as a family, for Jesus Christ said: "For where two or three are gathered together in my name, there am I in the midst of them."[1] At her insistence, we prayed

1. Matthew 18: 20 (KJV).

about it that evening, and to our surprise, God gave us the answer that selfsame night: I had a vision in which the Lord made it clear that before I was born, I was destined to be a missionary to the people of Bandiaterra—a fearsome cannibalistic nation that desperately needs to hear and receive the gospel. There has been no Christian missionary courageous enough to lay down his life and share the love of Jesus Christ with the Bandiaterran, because of numerous reports of cannibals roaming the island. The Lord commanded me to fear nothing and assured me that Archangel Gabriel— the strongest and most feared angel—will be dispatched to protect me, just like Michael has been delivering your notes to me since the beginning of our correspondence. Upon sharing the vision with my wife, she confirmed it by saying that the Lord had also spoken unto her last night, stating that she was handpicked to be my aid in a very important mission to evangelize a certain cannibalistic island called Bandiaterra. We then shared the news with our children and prayed together about it once more, and we all felt at peace with it.

I resigned from my job the following day, and on that Sunday, before I could even open my mouth and share the news with my church family, Brother Absalom Rehoboam phoned me and said, "So, are you going to be obedient to the Lord's calling?" Stunned, I asked him how he knew about it. He chuckled and invited me join him at the Kempinski Hotel after the morning service. I left church at the conclusion of the service and excitedly went to meet him, and at the closure of the meeting, he informed me that I was offered a full-ride scholarship to The Gate of the Lord Bible College, where I will be trained to become a missionary to the people of Bandiaterra. I am now at peace because there is no shadow of doubt creeping into my mind about my decision in resigning my job—all is well now. The Seminary is located in Bédogo, Logone Occidental and offers housing, meals, health care, and a stipend to my entire family while I am completing the disciple-ship training. Moreover, the School and EET N*18 church have set funds aside for my future mission work in Bandiaterra. Praise the Lord!

Dear brother, I would like to finish this letter on these notes, and would like to once again express my infinite gratitude to you for leading me to Christ! I grow in love with him daily, and his affection gets sweeter day after day. I never thought that my life could be fulfilling beyond mea-sure with the Lord, and I never fathomed how great a calling God had in store for me. Had I not known you, I would have never obeyed the Lord in his calling, and I would have died in ignorance and sin. Now, I know that nothing happens by chance with the Lord, for he preordained my destiny before I was conceived in my mother's womb. What a mighty God we serve indeed, that he would take the vilest of sinners like me, save me, sanctify me, and give me a divine mandate as his ambassador! May the name of the Lord be praise forever and ever!

Please keep me in your thoughts as I endeavor to get my training and become an ambassador of the Lord to the people of Bandiaterra.

Your brother in Christ,
Marawi.

Tuesday, June 3, 1997
1517 Year Zero BCE Road
Paradise, God's Kingdom

Dearest Brother in Jesus Christ,

Blessed indeed is the Lord Almighty who has favorably looked upon us, two friends, lost in sin, desirous to know the truth!

Blessed be the Lord for allowing you to develop the desire to know the truth and the will to challenge God to reveal himself to you!

Blessed be the Lord for appointing me to be a liaison between you and himself!

Blessed be the Lord who saved your soul from the trap of the devil who wanted to snatch your soul and make it dwell forever in the lake of fire!

Blessed be the Lord who cured your diverse maladies and opened your eyes on the limitlessness of his power!

Blessed be the Lord who reunited you with your wife and children!

Blessed be the Lord who sent his servant Absalom Rehoboam to you to be your mentor in faith!

Blessed be the Lord who put the appropriate words in the mouth of his servant, Pastor Njéla Timothy during your first church service!

Blessed be the Lord who brought conviction in your heart, and that of your doctor, family, and peers!

Blessed be the Lord who called you to be a missionary to the lost and gospel-thirsty people of Bandiaterra!

Blessed be the Lord who burdened your heart to be a missionary and confirmed it by the words of your wife!

Blessed be the Lord for giving you membership at EET N*18!

Blessed be the Lord for making The Gate of the Lord Bible College the venue for your training in biblical precepts!

Blessed be the Lord for making provision for your education and mission work with the people of Bandiaterra!

Blessed be the Lord for your obedience to his calling and fulfillment of your mission on Planet Earth.

May his name be blessed forever and ever. Amen!

I read your last letter with tears and rejoiced greatly for what the Lord has done in your life. I am now at peace for all my efforts throughout the years to bring you to Christ. It is indeed no coincidence that we met and became friends—it was ordained in divine eternity by God himself.

As soon as we received the news that you have not only decided to follow Jesus Christ, but resigned from your current position to answer the call of God Almighty to become a missionary, Brother Jephthah Abiathar convened the host of angels at a feast meant to celebrate your noble decisions. He sends you his most sincere congratulations and brotherly affection from his dwelling place in heaven. Needless to say, I am overjoyed and cease not to celebrate this milestone in your pursuit to know the Father at a much deeper level.

You have been obedient to what Jesus said: "The harvest truly is plenteous, but the labourers are few; Pray ye therefore the Lord of the harvest, that he will send forth labourers into his harvest."[2] Father God would like me to inform you that you are going to be the greatest evangelist, apologist, and theologian, the like of which, no one has ever seen or heard of since the time of C.S. Lewis, Charles Spurgeon, and Billy Graham. Through you, he will bring salvation to the people of Bandiaterra and many more across the globe who have never heard of Jesus Christ, and those who remain stiff-necked vis-à-vis the call of the Father to forgo their sinful ways and come to the table of salvation, for their soul thirsts and hungers for truth.

It's vitally important that you keep praying earnestly, for the task at hand is grand. The Enemy is aware of it and is going to do anything within his power to sabotage the calling of God on your life. I, even I, your friend Melchizedek, will not cease to intercede to the Father for your cause—just

---

2. Matthew 9:37–38 (KJV).

like I have been doing since the days in which my soul lived in the earthly domain. I am absent in body but present in spirit.

Dear brother, it has been an immense pleasure assisting you to discover the truth and watching the love that the Father lavishes upon his children on you. I will continue to be optimistic for your spiritual growth and will write you periodically to check on your spiritual progress and accomplishments for Christ in Bandiaterra—the land of depraved cannibals. In the meantime, feel free to reach out to the Father or myself through prayer and letters. I am overly excited for all that you shall accomplish for the Lord, and I look forward to chatting with you and sharing the marvels of heaven when the Lord calls you home at an appointed time.

Salutations to your born-again family and all the brethren who accepted Jesus Christ with you.

May the Lord continually bless you beyond measure.

Your brother,
Melchizedek.

www.ingramcontent.com/pod-product-compliance
Lightning Source LLC
Chambersburg PA
CBHW051836020726
47502CB00005B/1820